The Mythic Circle

#43: 2021

Victoria Gaydosik
Manager and Fiction Editor

Nolan Meditz
Poetry Editor

Phillip Fitzsimmons
Archivist

Table of Contents

Half-Title ii   Table of Contents iii   Submit-Info iv   Contributors v-vi   Introductions vii

Title	Creator	Type	Page
Cover Art: *Cthulu in the Morning*	Phillip Fitzsimmons	Image	Front
Stories Grow Larger in the Night	Sarah Berti	Poem	1
By Any Other Name	Leigh Ann Brook	Image	2
The Stable Keeper's Son: A Fairy Tale	Wesley Young	Story	3
Yet to be Revealed	Katherine Dubke	Poem	7
The Tale of the Troll Maiden and the Cobbler	David Gilman Frederick	Story	8
Sleep	Krista Canterbury Adams	Poem	12
Welcome to the Busty Wench	E. Clarence Peterson	Story	13
Toby Knotwise	Samantha Henze	Image	14
The Black Eyes of Ulspruth-Dimot	Lee Clark Zumpe	Story	15
Tricked by the Queen of Fey	Ella Walsworth-Bell	Story	18
Mythopoeic Triskelion	Phillip Fitzsimmons	Image	24
The Grim Morass	David Samuels	Story	25
Poseidon	Mark Rhodes-Taylor	Image	27
Emhain Ablach	Joshua S. Fullman	Poem	28
The Little Wild	Julian Grant	Story	30
Clover for Archivists	Phillip Fitzsimmons	Image	33
C.S. Lewis's Meditation over "The Book of the Leoun"	Joe R. Christopher	Poem	34
Talking Things over in Hospital	S. Dorman	Story	35
SunMoon	Phillip Fitzsimmons	Image	37
Amergin	David Sparenberg	Poem	38
Vargar	Yiming Zhao	Image	40
Vargar	Andoni Cossio	Story	41
Peredur in the Wasteland	Joe R. Christopher	Poem	42
SunMoon 2	Phillip Fitzsimmons	Image	45
The Legend of Halmonga	Hector Vielva	Story	46
Two Souls Upon a Shore	Geoffrey Reiter	Story	49
Bird in the Branches	Leigh Ann Brook	Image	51
The Three Kindreds	Jonathan Rolfe	Poem	52
Alrond and the Magic Fox	Evgeny A. Khvalkov	Story	53
Two in One	David Sparenberg	Vision	57
Sunflowers for OLA	Phillip Fitzsimmons	Image	57
Flowers in Glass for Tolkien	Phillip Fitzsimmons	Image	59
Taliessen in the Rose Garden	Joseph Thompson	Image	60
Wood Witches	Krista Canterbury Adams	Poem	61
How the Dryad and the Naiad Got or Didn't Get Together	Kevan Kenneth Bowkett	Story	62
The Holy Green of Time	David Sparenberg	Poem	68
Holly in the New Millennium	Susan Cornford	Story	69
Rose Print	Leigh Ann Brook	Image	70
You Passed Me the Story	Sarah Berti	Poem	70
Hummingbird	Phillip Fitzsimmons	Image	Back

Access audio files of these stories and poems for free at the Digital Archives of The Mythic Circle *after August 1, 2022, at https://dc.swosu.edu/mcircle/; till then, purchase a paper copy through Amazon Kindle or the Mythopoeic Society.*

The Mythic Circle

#43: 2021

Information for Aspiring Contributors

The Mythic Circle solicits original fantasy-inspired stories and poems from the membership of the Mythopoeic Society and from the larger world—anyone may contribute, but we give first consideration to our membership. We are also looking for original visual art contributions in the form of jpeg or other suitable file formats.

A small literary magazine, *The Mythic Circle* is published electronically and for print-on-demand by the **Mythopoeic Society**, an organization which celebrates the work of J. R. R. Tolkien, C. S. Lewis, Charles Williams, and the other Inklings. These innovative writers drew upon the rich tradition of imaginative speculative narratives and returned fantasy to a respectable place in serious literature, and we carry on in their tradition. An affordable annual membership in the Society is available at http://www.mythsoc.org/join.htm.

The editors look mostly for original work by authors following the mythic tradition; this *can* include a certain amount of commentary and allusion to the works of other mythic authors (though such allusions and commentary are not necessary). However, the editors do not wish to see "fan fiction" such as stories that make use of characters, settings, or images from works by living or recent authors or artists or any works still under copyright.

Submissions and letters of comment should be e-mailed to mythiccircle@mythsoc.org. Contributors may also join the SWOSU Digital Commons, the archival repository of the Mythopoeic Society, and use the submission portal there, located at the following URL: https://dc.swosu.edu/cgi/submit.cgi?context=mcircle. Joining the Digital Commons will also provide extensive statistical feedback to contributors about worldwide downloads.

As a small literary and arts publication, we do not pay cash for contributions. The copyright for works published in *The Mythic Circle* remains with the author or artist, except for the specific rights given for publication in *The Mythic Circle*, for future reprints of a particular issue in print or electronic (including online) formats, and for distribution of *The Mythic Circle* to third party database partners. Our full copyright statement can be found at https://dc.swosu.edu/mcircle/policies.html - rights.

Our Contributors

Krista Canterbury Adams lives in Columbus, Ohio. Her influences include Algernon Blackwood, Anne Rice, Hilda Doolittle, Sylvia Plath, and Anne Sexton. She is a published poet, as well as a member of the SFPA. Her work appears in *Altered Reality Magazine, The Dark Sire, Collective Realms, Carmina Magazine, CC&D, Kelp Journal, BFS Horizons, The Fifth Di…, Illumen,* and *Gingerbread House Literary Magazine,* among others.

Sarah Berti is a mythmaker, ghostwriter, and editor at BrightLeafLiterary.com, and the author of the *Helix Library Mythos,* excerpts at thehelixlibrary.com. Her poetry has been published in *Reliquiae Journal, RIC Journal,* and *Luna Arcana.* She can be found in her off-grid sanctuary in the precambrian wilderness of Ontario, Canada, under the stars.

Kevan Kenneth Bowkett has been in the Canadian Reserves, washed dishes, planted trees, sold door-to-door, slept in an igloo, and run for Parliament. He's lectured at universities and worked in a daycare. His play *Time's Fancy: The War of King Henry V and Joan of Arc* was shown at the Winnipeg Fringe Theatre Festival in 2017. His work has appeared in *Mythprint,* the *Manitoba Eco-Journal,* and earlier editions of *The Mythic Circle.* His recent books (2020) include two fantasies, *The City of Sapphires* and *Seachild* (Volume One), the latter set in the fabled land of Cothirya (and available on Amazon).

Leigh Ann Brook is a Music Education major at SWOSU and is currently completing her teacher candidacy. She has had a passion for art and music since middle school and completed an AP studio art course her senior year of high school. Her future goal is to become a band director of a successful program.

Joe R. Christopher has had one book of poems published by a standard publisher and a hundred or so individual poems in journals. He also has had over half a dozen books of other sorts appear from standard publishers, including a couple on C. S. Lewis. In his retirement, he is trying to turn some of the papers he read at meetings into publishable form-as well as writing more poems.

Susan Cornford is a retired public servant living in Perth, Western Australia, with pieces published or forthcoming in *365 tomorrows, AHF Magazine, Akashic Books Fri Sci-fi, Altered Reality Magazine, Antipodean Science Fiction, Corner Bar Magazine, Frost Zone Zine, Fudoki Magazine, Theme of Absence* and *The Were-Traveler.*

Andoni Cossio (UPV/EHU) is working on a PhD dissertation entitled *The Evolution of J. R. R. Tolkien's Ecological Perspective through the Portrayal of Trees and Forests: From* The Hobbit *to* The Lord of the Rings , financed by the Basque Government and by the research group REWEST (IT-1026-16), funded by the Basque Government and the University of the Basque Country (UPV/EHU). His publications focus on nature and medieval influences in Tolkien's oeuvre, and he has organized seven international conferences in Spain on the Inklings.

S. Dorman writes science fiction. Her essays have appeared in publications such as *Extrapolation, An Unexpected Journal, Mythlore* and *Caelum et Terra,* and online in *Mere Orthodoxy* and *Superversive Inklings.* She writes allusive biblical fan fiction, satire, and rural town-in-transition Maine novels, holds an MA in humanities from CSUDH, and has authored Maine creative nonfiction—*Maine Metaphor*—books published in series by Wipf & Stock.

Katherine Dubke delights in discovering the magical in the mundane and seeks to reflect this theme in her writing. She received her BA in Humanities and Fine Arts at Concordia University Irvine and her MA in Children's Literature at KSU.

Phillip Fitzsimmons is the Reference and Digitization Librarian at the Al Harris Library at SWOSU in Weatherford, OK. He serves as the archivist for the Mythopoeic Society at https://dc.swosu.edu/mythsoc/. He has also been published/presented on the works of J.R.R. Tolkien, C.S. Lewis, Owen Barfield, and the Inklings. He began making stained glass about 20 years ago.

David Gilman Frederick published his short story "Leap of Faith" in the current (February/March) issue of the *Scarlet Leaf Review.* Previously, he has published with FunDead Publications and the Japanese Society of Writers, Editors, and Translators. His novella, *Trolls,* is available on Amazon.

Joshua S. Fullman is Professor of English at Faulkner University, where he teaches courses in poetry, film, medieval literature, and serves as a Fellow in the Great Books Honors Program. His poetry has been recently published or is forthcoming in *Poesis, An Unexpected Journal,* and *The North American Anglican Review.*

Julian Grant is a filmmaker, educator, and author of strange short stories, outlaw poetry, full-length novels/non-fiction texts and outsider comix. A tenured Associate Professor at Columbia College Chicago, his work has been published by *Dark Fire UK, Quail Bell, Avalon Literary Review, Alternative History Magazine, Granfalloon, Altered Reality, Clever Magazine, Peeking Cat Literary Journal, CafeLit, Horla, Bond Street Review, Horror Sleaze Trash & Adelaide Literary Magazine* and others.

Samantha Henze is a character artist and illustrator from Boise, Idaho. She holds a Bachelor of Fine Arts degree from Boise State University.

Evgeny A. Khvalkov, PhD, is a Russian historian, medievalist, teacher, and researcher of the history of the Genoese and Venetian colonies in the Northern Black Sea region and of intercultural communications in the Old World of the late Middle Ages. He serves as Associate Professor of the Department of History of the Higher School of Economics in St. Petersburg.

E. Clarence Peterson is an author, designer, musician, and educator and holds a Masters' degree in Education with a focus on Deaf education and assistive technology. He resides now in Nebraska with his wife and son, where he pokes at projects half-finished and ends up watching old episodes of "Sherlock," "Key and Peele," and "Whose Line Is It Anyway?" at odd hours of the night instead.

Geoffrey Reiter is Associate Professor and Coordinator of Literature at Lancaster Bible College and Associate Editor at the website Christ and Pop Culture. He has published academic essays on such writers as George MacDonald, C. S. Lewis, Arthur Machen, and Peter S. Beagle. His work has previously appeared in *Mythlore* and *The Mythic Circle*, and his poetry and fiction has also appeared in the *Spectral Realms* and *Penumbra.*

Mark Rhodes-Taylor is an artist and illustrator working on paganism, mythology and history, although he is willing to tackle any subject matter. He was encouraged in this by successes with *Touchstone* magazine and *Pagan Dawn* and is currently working on a divination deck based on the theme of Egyptian mythology.

Jonathan Rolfe is a Catholic student from Newberg, Oregon. In Fall 2021 he starts his first year studying Latin and Greek at Hillsdale College in Michigan. He has studied Anglo-Saxon after the example of J. R. R. Tolkien, and hopes to become a professor of comparative historical linguistics.

David Samuels is a bartender in Los Angeles. He divides his time between writing and mastering the finer points of Gwent. Additional stories set in Euvael appear in *Silver Blade Magazine, Swords & Sorcery Magazine*, and several others. Check it out at storyscriptorium.com.

David Sparenberg, author of *CONFRONTING the CRISIS, Essays & Meditations on Eco Spirituality*, is an eco-poet, shamanic storyteller and teacher of existential ecosophy. He lives in Seattle, WA. His book is now available for pre-publication ordering through Amazon.

Joseph Thompson is a student at King's College London, studying for an MA in Christianity and the Arts. He is an author, artist, and blogger, who writes regularly about the Inklings on his blog at https://stepstotaniquetil.com/ with a strong focus on the poetry of Charles Williams.

Hector Vielva graduated in History from the University of Valladolid and the University of Rouen-Normandy and later obtained master's degrees in Modern History from the University of Istanbul (Turkey) and in Literary Theory from the University of Salamanca. He has published several academic articles as well as some fictional tales. He is currently the Chair of the *Cátedra de Literatura Fantástica y Mitopoesis* and reviewer at *Revista Tártarus.*

Ella Wallsworth-Bell was brought up in a small village in Cornwall. She writes short stories that are modern takes on myth and magic and which are strongly rooted in place and time. Themes include mental health in small communities, disability and acceptance, coping with motherhood, and escape, both physical and metaphorical. Cornwall has a rich heritage of myth, and our stories are often linked to the sea.

Wesley Young is a writer, supply preacher, and high school literature teacher in Cochran, GA. He received his BA from UGA and his MFA from Reinhardt University. He lives in the middle Georgia area with his wife and two daughters.

Yiming Zhao is an independent artist currently living in Vitoria-Gasteiz, Spain. She holds a BA in economics from Northwest University in China and graduated from the GLS MA program at Duke University obtaining the Exemplary Master's Project prize in 2018. She uses both traditional and digital tools to create illustrations and sequential art in two-/three-dimensional formats. See more of her work at yimingzhao.myportfolio.com.

Lee Zumpe has been publishing horror, dark fantasy and speculative fiction since the late 1990s. His short stories and poetry have appeared in publications such as *Weird Tales, Space and Time* and *Dark Wisdom*; and in anthologies such as *Best New Zombie Tales* Vol. 3, *Through a Mythos Darkly, Heroes of Red Hook* and *World War Cthulhu.* His work has earned several honorable mentions in *The Year's Best Fantasy and Horror* collections. Visit http://www.leeclarkzumpe.com.

Editors' Introductions

Is it just us, or was 2020-2021 the worst year of the past hundred years? Infections, deaths, lockdowns, and quarantines too long for human endurance just kept on keeping on, intensified by squabbles between proponents of collective health measures (masks, vaccines, social distancing) on one side and of individual personal liberties, regardless of the social and health impact, on the other. But through it all, artists continued to think, dream, and produce new work.

As contributions rolled into the inbox, however, one couldn't help but notice the darker tone of many stories in particular. In this issue, #43, we have young people meeting and immediately falling into magically-induced danger (in "The Stable Keeper's Son," by Wesley Young, making a first appearance in *The Mythic Circle*), and we have old(er) people meeting and falling afoul of an ill-willed magical being (in "Tricked by the Queen of Fey," by Ella Walsworth-Bell, who also contributed a Cornwall story to issue #42). We have an adventurer striding into destruction (in "The Grim Morass," by David Samuels), and another leaping into danger and coming out the other side (in "The Black Eyes of Ulspruth Dimot," by long-time contributor Lee Clark Zumpe). We have tales of that universal transition from life to death which constitutes a kind of magic, or at the very least a mystery (in "Talking Things Over in Hospital," by S. Dorman—a continuation of her series of conversations between C. S. Lewis and Mark Twain, and in "The Little Wild," by Julian Grant). We have the conniving antics of a would-be trickster in the snippet "Welcome to the Busty Wench," by E. Clarence Peterson, which has been adapted as the initial episode of a YouTube series. And we have a struggle for survival, difficult enough for castaways facing only nature as an opponent, but made infinitely more threatening by the opposition of an unhinged mage (in "Two Souls on a Shore," by Geoffrey Reiter).

But all is not despair and dying and trickery! We have a number of old anad new folk tales from different parts of the world: from Spain, readers can enjoy the beast fable (of a sort) of "Vargar," an award-winning tale by Andoni Cossio, or the place-spirit story of "The Legend of Halmonga," by Hector Vielva; and from Russia, Evgeny Khvalkov brings us "Alrond and the Magic Fox"—all of us should be so lucky as to meet with such a fox! We also have two modern versions of folk tale romances: "How the Naiad and the Dryad Got or Didn't Get Together," by Kevan Kenneth Bowkett (another repeat contributor), and "The Tale of the Troll Maiden and the Cobbler," by David Gilman Frederick, inspired, perhaps, by the myth of Hades' kidnapping of Persephone. And we have a quick view of the magic world intersecting with global climate change in "Holly in the New Millennium," by Susan Cornford (all the way from Australia).

This year, we have expanded our poetry selections over last year's edition, the first by the new editors of *The Mythic Circle*. We offer, for our readers' enjoyment, two poems by Joe R. Christopher ("C.S. Lewis's Meditation over "The Book of the Leoun" and the long ballad "Peredur in the Wasteland"); Joe has contributed to *The Mythic Circle* since it was founded in 1987. David Sparenberg has nearly as long of a record with our journal, this year bringing us a commemoration, in "Amergin," of Ireland's legendary first poet, a celebration, in "The Holy Green of Time," of Tom Bombadil, and an ecosophic prose-poem in "Two in One." New or less-frequently-heard voices include the meditations on story-telling of Sarah Berti ("Stories Grow Larger in the Night" and "You Passed Me the Story") and two studies of the power of the natural world from Krista Canterbury Adams in "Sleep" and "Wood Witches." Katherine Dubke takes inspiration from J. R. R. Tolkien in "Yet to be Revealed." Jonathan Rolfe contributes "The Three Kindreds," commemorating the peoples of Middle Earth in varying meters, including a verse in alliterative meter for the dwarves. And finally, Joshua S. Fullman provides a study of old King Arthur in captivity in Avalon, pressured by Morgan Le Fay to accept his chains, in "Emhain Ablach."

The appearance of our journal has been greatly enhanced by the visual elements provided by contributors this year. We have a stained glass theme, announced by the cover images and re-emphasized throughout with smaller images displaying mythic elements, courtesy of the Archivist for the Mythopoeic Society, Phillip Fitzsimmons. But we also include pencil drawings by Marc Rhodes-Taylor, Joseph Thompson, and Leigh Ann Brook, a vivid portrait of the protagonist in "Welcome to the Busty Wench," by Samantha Henze, a custom illustration by Yiming Zhao for the story "Vargar," and two views of roses in different media by Leigh Ann Brook.

It would not be possible to produce this journal without extra help, and the editors would like to recognize the contributions and expertise of Diane Fitzsimmons, Dr. Brian Rickel, and Dr. Denise Landrum Geyer for assistance in mastering the mysteries of page numbering in MS Word, and of Jillian Drinnon in assembling the components of the front and back covers. The Steward for Social Media of the Mythopoeic Society, Alicia Fox-Lenz, provided an effective background image for the front cover. Many thanks to them all! And best wishes to our readers and our contributors for a year of good health and an end to the Covid-19 pandemic.

Victoria Gaydosik, Professor Emerita
Nolan Meditz, PhD and Assistant Professor

Aspiring Contributors:

Send stories, poems, and images (.docx/pdf/jpeg) to
mythiccircle@mythsoc.org

OR

Enroll with the Digital Commons at SWOSU at

< https://dc.swosu.edu/ >

AND

Download Back Issues of *The Mythic Circle* at

< https://dc.swosu.edu/mcircle/ >

A Poem by Sarah Berti

Stories Grow Larger in the Night

in the morning fold your wings but in the dark
go out

to where the story is seeded from the twisted open mouths of salt-bound monsters

and the night Travels
at a different rate than the day

bear their intimate stare and cold-fingered shuffling of scores of ill-fitting tales familiar garments of
horror

choose the particular pain-body
to mask
what you were Telling
when the First Fire went out
and the original story too bright to see got reclothed in shadows

to be retold by a phalanx of phantoms across time
deformed voices
designed to distort

remember
across the membrane
until what we craft in the night when we cannot see the way

will become a Legend

for the ouroboros tale of shadow and light is singular
and double and everlasting

and the night despite its divisions

cannot be divided

By Any Other Name by Leigh Ann Brook

The Stable Keeper's Son: A Fairy Tale

By Wesley Young

Malkin's riders were venturing farther and farther across the border—nearly, the scouts reported, to the River Sils, which was the easternmost edge of the dominion of Welborne. The King of Welborne spent much time in council, listening to the varied advice of the elders. "Strong magic. You must appeal to strong magic," said one. "Strong weapons, larger armies, that's the way," said another. "The only help for us against Malkin," said a third, the oldest of them all, "is the Deep Magic, greater than which no man knows. The Sprites can show the way."

For Filgrie, the stable boy, these councils in the castle meant less work in the stables. Over the last ten days, King Nobley had ridden only once. And so it was that one early morning, Filgrie's dad saddled a tall, white mare, then said to his son, "She needs to be ridden. Take her out a while, no galloping, and do not go near the river."

"Yes, Father," Filgrie said. He mounted and was off with a wide smile. He led the beautiful animal along Market Lane, to avoid the river, until he reached Grinson's Meadow, and there he turned toward the hills where the townspeople pastured their sheep. Just as he crossed the stone bridge at the end of town, out of the ground rose a Sprite. Filgrie pulled the reins and halted. The creature breached the earth, rippling the dirt away like a wave of water. She—for it seemed clearly female—stood full height on the now solid ground, the grass beneath her feet showing no sign of having been disturbed. With a voice like rain on a soldier's shield, she sang.

> *Fortune rise and fortune fall,*
> *Why is fortune here to call?*
> *You'll ride and reel past briar and brook,*
> *But we'll do something to your look.*

The creature was twice as tall as Filgrie, and had white hair and a white robe with shoes of white glass. Her garments moved like water. Welborne legends often included these beings, which is how Filgrie recognized it right away, though in the stories the Sprites were thought to be much smaller. The tales were accurate, however, about their use of rhymes and riddles, and every citizen of Welborne knew to take these seriously.

Something in her eyes frightened Filgrie, and he kept trying to look away, but found he couldn't manage for more than a few moments. Turn his gaze where he might, within a breath or two he snapped back to stare into the deep, pupil-less eyes. He waited for the second riddle—Sprite's always sing twice a day, lightning and thunder—but nothing came.

Then the creature looked down at the ground just in front of Filgrie's horse. She clapped her hands together. The ground, again behaving like water, rolled in a cresting wave that washed the horse high up, then tossed it back. Filgrie was on the ground in a moment, striking hard on his back, trying in a tangle to get to his feet. The horse had fallen too, and would have crushed Filgrie except that it landed a little to his left.

The boy was just steadying himself on his knees when the second wave hit, soil and sod like a wave on the seashore, this time breaking right on him. He closed his eyes and tumbled backward in the wash. When he opened them again, all was level grass and empty pasture. The king's horse was getting up. The Sprite was gone.

Filgrie's face was covered with grainy mud that bothered his eyes. He rubbed them, which only let more mud in and made things worse. It was hard to see. He staggered to his horse and mounted, ungracefully. Just as he situated himself in the saddle, the mare took off at a blistering gallop. Never had any of the horses under his father's care done anything besides obey, but now this animal was fully wild.

Filgrie talked to it, called to it, pulled on the reins, yelled for help, all to no effect. His eyes were watering and stinging, and he could hardly see at all. He considered jumping off, but could not bring himself to do it, so instead he leaned far forward and held on with all his strength.

***

Far away, on the other side of the River Sils, Lithe said goodbye to the chickens and decided to take the Sils Trail home so she could have a look at the river. She longed for a quiet moment to sit by the old waterwheel. With her basketful of eggs held in one arm, and a white flower in the other, she walked toward the lowering sun.

Her parents would rather her come straight home from the chicken roost. As frontier farmers homesteading in the woods between Welborne and Malkin, the family was brave by necessity, but also cautious. The chicken chore was the farthest Dad allowed Lithe to venture unaccompanied. She liked the distance. Her love for her family was complemented by her love for solitude in the deep woods, and it was a thirst for this solitude that led her now to her favorite spot in all the world.

When Lithe was five years old, and their family only one year on the farm, her father took her and her baby brother to the River Sils to show them the ruins of the dwarf's waterwheel, used in the last century for everything from grinding grain to polishing gold for Welborne's castle. She loved the place immediately. They sat on the banks in silence as the sun sank in the west and the magic of twilight rose from the earth. It was that day that they saw the Fairy Fleet— the three dozen tiny vessels, some with sails and some with paddles, manned by the tiniest, playfulest, most beautiful glowing creatures Lithe ever imagined. Despite her returning to the same spot as often as she might, she never captured a second glimpse of that spectacle. But the way her heart felt that first day, the memory of that memory, drove her back and back again, washed to the banks by the ever-welling hope inside her. She was too young to know that the Fairy Fleet is never found when it is looked for.

Not far from twilight, she reached the spot. She hung her egg basket on a low limb, stuck the flower in her hair, and sat down on the grassy bank. Across the river the fireflies sparked from within the darkness of the wood. There was deep forest in all directions. The dwarf's wheel sat unmoving, and she watched the water trickling over the cups, tinkling into the river like diamond drops in a sea of glass. She could see fish in the clear, flowing stream below, chasing one another in their evening games.

Then she heard the hoofs, thundering across the river, sending up swarms of glowing fireflies. The rider came into view as the horse dashed wildly through the trees. It ran upriver until out of Lithe's sight, then the thundering grew louder as it doubled back and bolted along the bank. The rider was leaning forward and shouting at the animal. The river was not at all wide, and she could hear him clearly. He was only a boy. She sat as frozen as the waterwheel.

Suddenly the creature dug in its hoofs and tossed the rider over its head and into the river, about midways across. Lithe sprang to her feet and ran down the hill to the water's edge. Kicking off her shoes, she rushed into the water.

The boy came up, splashing and spluttering.

4

"Here!" she called, wading farther out to about waist deep. "Here, swim toward me. There you go. It's alright."

He paddled toward her, saying nothing. When he was near enough, she reached out and took one of his hands and held it tightly in hers. His face was covered in dark mud, almost black, and she thought it strange that his plunge into the water had not washed any off. She considered that it might be some sort of mask the boy was wearing, but if so, it was an odd mask, a liquid one, slipping and dripping down his face. He gained his footing and stood up in the shallow water. Then he pulled his hand from hers and plunged his head into the river, rubbing his face below the water, both hands working rapidly. He rose, and she saw that half the mud was gone. Down he went again, and again wiped and scrubbed. When he surfaced this time, Lithe saw his fully revealed features.

A tight, clipped gasp escaped from her throat. Her chest tightened, and, hardly knowing what to do, she dropped into the water, falling onto both knees, her head the only thing above the surface. She bowed as low as she could without submerging. The flower fell from her hair and floated downstream.

"I am sorry, I didn't know, I am—"

"What are you doing?" the boy asked.

"I'm sorry, I've never, and I didn't know, you see, because your face was covered."

"Didn't know what? Stand up, let's get out of the river. Why are you down there?"

Before she could answer a new noise came from the woods behind them, faintly rising from the now darkened forest on the girl's side of the river. Hoofbeats. These grew rapidly louder, and Lithe could tell they were from many horses. She stood, fearing these might be the Malkinians. The evening was darkening to night. She scanned the bank for a place to hide.

"They're coming on quick. Let's get to that millhouse," the boy said.

"Yes," she answered, still awestruck. Lithe had recognized his face immediately. This rider who had been tossed into the river was the Prince of Welborne, the only son of the king. Lithe had seen the royal family twice in her life, the most recent at last year's Festival, where she had watched this prince parade by in the great procession. She never doubted that the boy now with her in the river was this same royal personage.

The pair ran the sludging and awkward trudge enforced by knee deep water. The fireflies from within the wood were ablaze and swarming, yellow lights darting here and there among the shadowed trees.

"Hurry," the supposed prince shot out in a half whisper. "They're close."

Now splashing along in ankle deep water, now on the grass of the bank, they sprinted toward the shelter of the mill. Twenty paces to go. Their own footfalls blended with the thunder of the hoofs that grew ever louder. Ten paces. Lithe was panting. Almost there.

Then from the blackness among the trees an even darker blackness erupted. A dozen riders on charcoal horses wearing the black and red robes of Malkin shot out of the forest and cut off the children's flight, stopping in front of the waterwheel.

The princely boy reached out and took Lithe's arm in a firm grasp. "It's alright," he said. "We'll be alright. Just follow me," and he began walking backward slowly, keeping his eyes forward on the riders.

"Yes, sire," Lithe said, comforted by his royal courage.

"Why do you call me—"

"Halt!" a terrible voice roared from behind them. They both snapped around to find their retreat cut off. Five Malkinian soldiers, on foot, had silently crept in and made an impassable wall.

The riders by the mill drew nearer, tightening the distance. One open lane remained, straight away toward the trees. Lithe's knees tensed for a last desperate bolt, but before she could make the dash, more riders materialized out of the tree line, and the entrapment was complete.

"Take him," said one dark rider, a voice like a war drum.

Two of the dismounted soldiers came up behind Filgrie and took his arms.

"The Prince of Welborne," continued the black rider. "This is a fortunate turn, indeed. And all unguarded in the forest."

"Oh, you forget," another shadow jeered, "he's got his bodyguard there."

This taunt drew uproarious laughter from the Malkinians. Lithe's knees nearly gave way, and only by a great effort did she keep from collapsing to the ground. She looked to the prince who was looking right back at her with desperate eyes. The look reminded her, somehow, of her younger brother. This sparked an idea.

"Wait!" she called out, pitifully. "Wait, you've made a mistake." A tear swelled to breaking and trickled down her nose. She choked a moment, then continued with her speech, which she thought was a complete lie. "This is not the prince. This is my brother. Folks say they look alike. We are frontier farmers. He was helping me with the chickens. The eggs are just there, over there, on the bank," and she pointed to where she had left the basket. Her knees were betraying her again, and she could say no more. When she looked at the prince, she found his eyes looking less afraid and more confused.

"Silence!" the rider roared. "You will not talk your way out of this, dear one. We've as big of plans for you as for him, perhaps even more sporting."

At these words Lithe could stand no longer, and she fell to the grassy ground in a heap, which elicited another wild laugh from the onlooking soldiers.

Filgrie stood bewildered by the scene, but his mind was beginning to piece together the girl's words, and the Malkinians', and also the cryptic chant of the Sprite. He couldn't know for sure, not without some way to see his reflection, but he had enough of a hunch to try something desperate.

"She lies!" he lied. "Hear the prince's words. She is no sister of mine. I have never seen her before, and I will let no subject of mine die on my lands. Let her go, and I will leave with you peacefully. You have captured the Prince of Welborne, be content with that."

For a frozen moment, nothing happened.

"What is more," Filgrie went on, "I will write letters to my father, the king, saying that I have deserted Welborne of my own accord. Your taking me by force will cause war, but by my word it can be prevented. Only let this girl go!"

The leader spurted out a short laugh, but then fell into silence. The other Malkinians stared at him. After some time, he spoke. "Let's go. We have what we want."

"But—" one of Filgrie's captors began to complain.

"I said let's go! Leave the girl."

Two soldiers snatched the princely stable boy to a horse and tossed him, chest downward, in front of the saddle. Lithe, still in a heap on the turf, could only watch as the army trotted off into the forest. Filgrie looked back at her, gave a strange smile, and then disappeared into the night.

The girl felt she would never move again. The evening's shift from eggs and Fairy Fleets to wild horses and wicked riders was overwhelming. Her spirit reeled. She collapsed farther, lying now on her side, and closed her eyes against the world.

She assumed she awoke in a dream. The ground was moving. Not shaking like an earthquake, but rolling like the ripples of a lake. She sat up, wide eyed. An enormous figure stood before her, something like a huge woman, glowing in the night with a pale lunar luminescence. The waterwheel, which had been frozen her whole life, was spinning rapidly. She wondered how that could be, and as she looked up at the looming, glowing figure, she wondered what sort of danger she was in now, and she began to cry.

"Where did they take him?" the creature asked in a voice like running water.

"The prince?"

"The boy. Where did they take him?"

"To Malkin, I suppose," Lithe sobbed.

"No, I mean where was he standing when they took him? Where was he when he saved you?"

"There," she said, pointing, "right there next to where you're standing."

The Sprite looked down. The ground was still wavering like the surface of a windblown lake. Rather than stoop, the creature remained standing and sank into the earth until her arms were able to reach the grass. With one motion she yanked a handful of turf and held it tightly in her hand. Then she slowly began to sink even farther down, chanting as she went.

> *Deep devotion, ancient wine,*
> *Is there Magic Deep as thine?*
> *None can match, oh wondrous thought,*
> *Salvation sacrifice has bought.*

A Poem by Katherine Dubke
Yet to be Revealed
After J. R. R. Tolkien

Rest beside this mound of stones
As sun descends from clouded throne.
See his silken threads of gold,
Diffuse the light he ever holds;
Royal robes worn by his grace
Adorned by train of rose and lace.
Sky attends the sun's advance
Until he sets from the expanse.
Speak, while clouds are grey and still
and as we linger on this hill.
What is it from life you seek?
The glory of the sun is weak
Compared to what I see in you:

A fire of prismatic hue

Smolders in your steady eyes;
Unlike the sun, it never dies.

Reveal to me your solemn vows.
The stones and I bear witness now.

The Tale of The Troll Maiden and the Cobbler

David Gilman Frederick

Once, in the lands across the sea, there was a cobbler. Unremarkable as such an occupation may be here, in those lands it is one of high esteem. They have rugged cliffs to scale, unknown steppes to cross, jagged boulders, spiny hedgehogs, mudflats, cacti, flints, vines, thorns—much of that land, I have heard, is picturesque, with sweeping vistas and forests that anticipate the colors of the sunset. But much is wild, unconquered, untamed, flinty, and hard on the soles of feet. Settlements are sparse, and skilled craftsmen hard to come by. So, once there was a cobbler. He was a modest man, yet he was a virtuoso at his trade. When asked, he said his Helper spoke to him. He would quiet himself and his environment, and the Helper would speak him soft, gentle words in his ear, or in his mind, and he would know exactly what to do—the right grade leather in so many layers, the rivets placed here and here, the treated cork carved in just such a curve for support. In time, even those on the fashionable Eastern Seaboard would turn to him for the sensibility and longevity of his shoes, and for the cunning, subtlety of art, and discretion which they implied. When settlers ranged farther inland, they too would seek out the necessity that was a pair of the famous cobbler's lifetime guaranteed, virtually impregnable shoes.

"The Helper," he said, and smiled. And he did have a voice that guided him. He had since childhood. It told him where to cut, where to fasten. For a while he had thought it the bashful presence of some small, fantastical man—a Tree Man, a Mushroom Man—who always kept just behind him, just around his back, over his shoulder. Yet as the years went on, he realized the Helper was none other than himself. He caught himself mouthing sets of words on both sides of his silent conversations—both his words and those of the Helper. They were just him, inside his mind, and he knew it. The cobbler was alone.

So it was, alone one day, that the cobbler walked beyond the bounds of his village, and into the bright forests that cover those lands—forests of maple, and ash, oak, and elm. It was a brisk morning, fit for movement, and the cobbler strode farther than he was accustomed to. There are few people, still, in the colonies, on the edge of the frontier, but the aboriginal trolls have lived among those hills and valleys since time immemorial, and their comings and goings have carved paths like rills throughout the countryside. It was following one of these, and testing his new patent soles against the delicious crackling of fallen leaves, that the cobbler heard the sound of falling water, and a woman's voice in low harmony. Aware that he walked on troll-paths, the cobbler's first thought was silence and cover. Trolls don't climb trees, he knew; they hated to break the connection between their feet and the soil. So he launched into the nearest oak tree with a pre-adolescent enthusiasm. He sprang from branch to branch, less concerned for sound now that he felt himself protected and out of reach. Neither the sound of the water nor the singing paused or changed.

The cobbler could see from his new vantage that there was a conceivable path from branch to branch if he was brave enough to take it, from oak to ash to wandering maple. If he made boldly along the crowns of the canopy, he could move closer in toward the crash of waters and perhaps overlook them like a catamount without risking detection from below. He tested his grip and flexed his soles. The tread on the new patent shoes held steady. See what you can, the Helper whispered behind his ears.

It took the better part of an hour to reach it, but all at once he found himself overlooking a deep gully, a wrinkle in the woods all but hidden beneath a curtain of birch and willow leaves. At the base of the gully the waters formed a deep pool, dark as sapphire and still but for where two separate cataracts trickled and churned. Along the far side of the water there was a lip, a ledge, just high enough to avoid the general splashes, from where licorice ferns waved back at the waters, cheering their glory.

It was a beautiful scene. The cobbler was so struck with its perfection that it threw him into a deep melancholy. For he would like to share it with someone, but he had no one he could bring here, this far out of the village. He had no one with whom acquaintance was any deeper than a business transaction. Bemoaning himself within his mind, talking to the Helper, he almost missed the change that had occurred below. The sound brought him back just in time to see a troll-maiden emerge from the bottom of the pool and break through to the surface.

As you know, the aboriginals of those lands all have this gift, that they can dig, or burrow, feet-first, at a dizzying speed. Presumably this is how the troll-maiden had emerged; she had been deep beneath the soil and composite stones that lined the base of the pool, but now she burst up and through, leaving a red cloud of disturbed earth billowing behind her to muddy the waters. She stepped, or swam, to one of the cataracts, and spun beneath its frothy force, the mass of her yellow hair splitting into sundry locks. All the while she hummed a low tune. She was completely naked.

Trolls are large, as a rule, and this one was no exception. Despite what you may have heard, however, they are also well-proportioned. There is a grace to their strength and motions, a feline comeliness to their fair hair and strangely pale eyes. At worst, and absent of the mud that for them is ubiquitous, they are said not to look so different from us, or from the colonists themselves.

The cobbler watched as, naked and clean, the troll-maiden lifted herself to the embankment, the crystal waters dripping like sparks from her toes as they emerged from the pool. She lay down in a shaft of sunlight. Her limbs splayed artlessly, her hair radiating out in thick wet bands. The skin of her massive chest and shoulders glistened into a smear of light, as if it was the sole purpose of the sun. Her eyes were closed and a smile was on her lips. In time her breathing slowed to a snore. She had fallen asleep, undisturbed, unaware of the smaller human perched above, watching her.

Carefully, carefully, the cobbler inched his way backward along the interlocking, aerial road provided by the branches. Finding the foot path once more, he ran as quickly and as quietly as he could back to town. Later he doubted he had closed his eyes the whole time, even to blink. When he finally did, he found her image there emblazoned, a blur of smiling light behind his eyelids.

Now the cobbler was a lonely man. He had few acquaintances and no friends in the small hamlet where he lived, and his closest relations were several days' journey away, far back along the Eastern Seaboard. He had come inland on his own, after he graduated from his apprenticeship, with only the Helper for company—and even then he knew it to be a hollow reflection of sound, a trick of the mind if not an outright affliction. I do not seek to justify him, but you must understand: Rules are raw out on the frontier, and it is far easier to see the difference between what one can do and what one must from here in the old world, where the ages have layered grace upon our human mistakes.

Until that day, the cobbler had never felt admiration for anyone, much less desire. But when he closed his eyes and thought of her beneath those falls, or lying beside them, snoring and glistening, he could think of nothing else. He closed his shop to the public, put his current orders aside, and for many days, he simply sat and thought of her.

At length the Helper awoke him from his reverie. It told him of intricate laces and complicated, fascinating buckles, puzzles of leather straps and nickel locks. Gradually beneath his hands there formed a shoe, at first a boot, and then a dainty slipper, so steadfastly wrought that it would age indefinitely and might be worn forever. Indeed, it was so cunningly cinched that once worn, it would be nearly impossible to take off. They were slippers of delicate emerald leather; they were faster than iron manacles. He dared not try them on himself, but he was a master craftsman, and he guessed her size to the width of a toenail. He remembered the wiggling and grasping of her toes while she lay and slept, and for a cloudy moment he was almost ashamed, but then with a sigh he realized they would always be free somewhere—for couldn't he see them here, bright as daylight on a mirror, inside his eyelids?

It had been several months by the time he retraced his steps to that pool and climbed once more with precious care along the leafy, branching highway. It was the later middle of autumn, and the weather had nearly turned, but the sun was still protesting the inevitable with every glorious set. He was not at all sure she would be there, but the Helper told him to try it. And, when at first he did not see her, the Helper told him to wait.

At last she appeared. A cloud of red dust flew sideways from among the ferns and gradually precipitated along the surface of the water. One moment she was not there; the next, she was the center of everything, the axis of the horizon, laughing in outward ripples around which the cobbler's world spun.

It seemed, to him, that she bathed for hours before settling onto the bank to rest. The Helper muffled and stilled his circulation as he waited for the muscles in her hips to relax, her telltale twitches, her snore. When at last the moment came, he crept stealthily, breathlessly, across an archway of willow and vining maple, until he landed softly by her feet.

In the space it took her eyelids to flicker open, he'd already slipped on and fastened the first of the little green shoes. She arched with her knees and her back, attempting to force her toes into the soil, but his clever slipper was too great an impediment for her right foot, and she lurched left with such force that her bare toes unearthed themselves again. Quick as he could, the cobbler wrapped his whole frame around her left leg and held on, determined to keep her above the surface. She kicked at him with her right, scratching his face with the clever nickel buckles, twisting and turning and threatening to drown him in the gully, but he was implacable. He slipped on the second shoe, cinched the tricky laces, and then released her back to the earth. She landed on her elbows with a thud and blew her feathery hair away from her eyes.

"Well," she said, sizing him up; "You've won that round. But I will win the next one."

By the time they made it back to his shop it was well past midnight. He had led her slowly, gently, like a newborn foal, for it was difficult for her to walk at all with a layer of foreign skin between herself and the earth. She never once tried to escape, though she did consider it, he was sure, for as he led her on he felt on several occasions a tension, a pause, a quick intake of breath. But then she relaxed and continued to allow him to lead her to his home.

He had thrown a blanket over her, not so much to keep her warm as to hide her nakedness and thus limit his shame. He needn't have worried, however; since there was no one about in the streets when they finally reached and crossed his bachelor's threshold. His shop was not far from others along the merchant's boulevard, but there were no watch or lanterners in his small town. The people knew each other; the trolls kept to themselves in the neighboring hills and were the peaceable sort.

Thus no one knew the cobbler had taken a troll-wife until the wrestling began. The din of their matches was prodigious and could be heard, at times, from before the first light in the morning until long after the shadows swallowed everything beyond the circles of light around the shops and houses that defined the Merchants' Boulevard. The milliner, passing by in midday, saw the walls shaking and thought the roof about to collapse. He froze in indecision, struck by the desire to help and the sure folly of rushing into an unstable building. Inside he heard splintering, shouting, and laughter; the frame continued to rattle, but the structure was firm, He decided to run for help, and returned with a small posse of other townsfolk, crowbars, torches, and buckets of water. The building continued to shudder and creak.

"Should we try to go in?" someone asked.

"Through the front door?" doubted another.

"Knock it in?" suggested a third.

But then a model wooden leg sailed through a window to their right. A few brave ones scrambled over and peered inside.

They saw, or said they saw, a tremendous woman hurl the cobbler against a chair, which collapsed beneath him. She leapt for him, to pin him down, but he rolled to the side and wrapped both arms around her knee, curbing her momentum so that she crashed into a cabinet of tools for curing leather. They said he laughed, and that she did too, flashing large, feral teeth before pouncing at him once more.

After that, the townsfolk left them alone. They wondered how anything of value might survive in the cobbler's shop, but it was his shop, and the people of the frontier are a quiet, independent sort. They left him to it.

At length it did settle down, and the cobbler began fulfilling his orders again. Within the space of a year, she had borne twins. Two years later, it was triplets, and then twins again. The cobbler's business barely slowed—for there was always work for him, such was his reputation—but he began to expand his house, building lean-tos and a second-story loft onto the back of his property.

She was seldom seen around town, for though they supposed she was his wife, she was also a troll, and she never sought the social affection they never proffered her. But some days she would lead her children through the market -- dressed, though barely, to the standards of the women of that country. And inevitably they would notice her shoes, her peculiar soft, delicate green slippers, with their intricate lace and enviable nickel buckles, and some of the women would sigh. They supposed these were the secret by which the cobbler had won her – though they could not fathom how close they hit the truth, nor how wide they missed.

The captive troll loved her children. They were always about her, perched on her shoulders, hanging from her shins, climbing her as if she were a large boned, blonde mountain. They rarely followed their father into the workshop, or into town when it was his turn to go to the market. They clung to her, and at home they ran around naked as she did, though unlike her they did not wear shoes.

And so it was one day they were lying on the carpet together, rolling on the floor, piled and wiggling, when the one plaiting her hair asked the question. "Mama," she said, "why don't you ever take off your slippers?"

For her the world stilled and grew cold, as cold and crisp as the waters beneath the cataract where she used to swim. But the children kept babbling and squirming around.

"I can't," she said eventually. "I cannot unknot the laces or unclasp the buckles. And the leather is too smooth to cut or tear." She traced a finger along the outside edge of a shoe, sadly.

"But we can do it, mama," the child said. Reaching out, she insinuated a finger underneath a strand of her mother's shoelace and pulled. The Troll-Woman felt tension release in a spasm all up and down the left side of her body. The child grinned, and with a twist, unlocked the seven buckles. The shoe peeled back and fell away.

Two more of her children had begun working on her other foot, but when she gave a gasp and cry, they stopped. They had never heard their mother make a sound that small before. They stared at her with trepidation.

"No," she urged them; "go on. Do it. Let's finish this match."

11

As soon as the second shoe slipped away, almost in one motion, she swept up the seven children in her arms and rushed through the front door into the street before her house. She didn't get dressed. She didn't close the door behind her.

Now the cobbler had just made a fine sale, and had gone down the road to the bakery to buy fresh rolls with his earnings. He was humming as he made his way back to his own shop, a low tune he had heard once somewhere, a happy memory of yellow, blue, and green that he couldn't quite place.

She saw him moments before he saw her himself, and she knew him though he was somewhat abstracted, not comprehending her appearance in the light of day, with fourteen additional naked limbs squirming and writhing within her grasp. She looked down at her feet.

They were too pale, too pink and purple, too soft against the compact soil from their years of confinement within the little green shoes. She would bleed, she was sure; it would hurt her to dig, and she would not recover for a long time. She looked up to meet his eyes; saw the consternation and concern. It was worth it.

She smiled at him, a bright, toothy smile, that would linger for days or years on the inside of his eyelids, burning brilliantly ever deeper into his mind. And then, with a grinding sound of stone against stone, in a flashing cloud of red dust, she was gone, down into the earth in the way of trolls, taking all seven of her children with her.

The cobbler never saw any of them again.

A Poem by Krista Canterbury Adams

Sleep

All night frowns down.
We listen to the spirit voices
Alive in the grove,
Voices so much like water
Moving over smooth stones.
We listen to the unearthly trees
High above in the dark—

"Sleep,"
Say the owls from the black branches,
"All things sleep at our feet."

This sleep,
A shower of leaves.
This sleep,
Winter melting
Into the trees.

Welcome to the Busty Wench

By E. Clarence Peterson

Episode 1—The Coppery Hint of Blood

Toby's step down from the coach was greeted by the damp embrace of cobblestone puddles. Deceptively deep and cold, they were none too fresh, either. Indeed, the distinct flavors of body odor, pig shit, and the coppery hint of blood were thick in the air. Ah, yes, civilization at last.

"Watch that first step, little man. It's a doozy." the coachman dryly observed from his wagon perch.

"You might've pulled forward another twenty rods to spare me this morass, good sir," Toby replied, mustering what manners he could. Mother had always stressed the importance of being nice. That, of course, being until it was time not to be nice.

"City guard won't let me go no farther," the coachman reflected. "They gotta search each wagon going into town, assess taxes, and look for contraband. We wouldn't want any undesirables making it into town, now, would we?"

"Certainly not, sir!" Toby hastily replied, unconsciously fingering the lockpicks hidden at his belt.

Looking two wagons ahead, Toby observed two of the city guard making a concerted effort to shake down a wide-eyed shepherd for a bribe at the city gate. And when the poor fellow produced none, the guard began snapping their gloves and speaking of cavity searches.

Oh no, this would not do. Stepping quietly to shadow, Toby assessed his options. City guards, as a rule, are notoriously corrupt and run their game on the common folk. However, they dare not impede the will of the rich and powerful.

Fingering his coin purse, Toby found it light. And judging by the crowd here assembled, there would be no juicy mark aching to be relieved of their burden of gold. There was, however, a person of interest.

Not two spots back, there stood a group of religious pilgrims, waving incense and chanting nonsense about giving Demeter her due. Foremost among the group loomed the mighty presence of a diminutive woman, who seemed to be the leader.

Slipping closer, Toby gleaned her name. It was Sister Maude. Oh, and she was a firebrand! And when one of her followers shouted "Amen, Sister Maude!" the outlines of a plan sprung to Toby's mind. So, stepping forward into the crowd, Toby raised his hands in rapturous repose, and projected "Amen, Sister Maude" in full theatrical voice. The flock, surprised by this unexpected boon, turned to face him.

"Who brings the crops which feed us?" he asked. The crowd, apparently not the sharpest of tacks, muttered moronic potentials such as "Farmer Brown?" or "The Fat Red Wagon?" Toby was forced to self-punctuate.

"Demeter," he concluded with a smack of his fist. "But who gets all the credit?" he whispered, with a conspiratorial lean.

"Jupiter!" he boomed, "for bringing the rain. Bacchus!" he cried, "for bringing the wine." "Neptune!" he wept, "for the meager returns of the sea."

Yet, who brings you the staple of wheat or the joy of the lima bean?" He paused for effect.

"Demeter, I say!" he burst, fist pumping to air. And this was indeed greeted by appreciative murmurs from the crowd.

"And she does so in silence, asking for nothing," he hushly reflected. Casting his eyes to ground, Toby whispered: "Giving of herself, humbly, with sincerity."

Nods of solemn agreement were noted in the crowd.

Building then to impending crescendo, he continued: "Caring not about all the praise we heap on the other gods, she does what must be done!"

"Amen, brother!" and various other slack-jawed shouts of agreement rose from the crowd.

"And you, Sister Maude, you are doing the gods' work. Spreading the virtues of Demeter. Bless you sister, bless you," he added with a tear in his eye.

At this point, the crowd was momentarily pushed aside by that wide-eyed shepherd and his flock of sheep, who apparently had been unsuccessful in their attempt to enter the city: The poor shepherd clutching his loosened pantaloons, and the city guards roaring with laughter.

"Well said, son," Sister Maude gushed. "It lifts my heart to hear young people like you so full of the bounty of Demeter," she added.

Toby realized that Sister Maude had mistaken him for human. This was not an uncommon mistake, as halflings do quite resemble younger humans when they choose not to wear facial hair. This error not hurting his case, Toby chose not to correct her.

"Yes, sister. Mother is a strong woman, like you. She taught me what's right."

"Have you come with your mother to bathe your feet in Demeter's fountain, son?" Sister Maude inquired.

"Mother asked me to find some flowers to lay there, but naught but dandelions could I find in the wild, and these flower merchants outside the wall are near criminal in their pricing!"

"Aye, the merchants inside the wall are no better, son! Your mother was wise to send you out into nature for an offering. This would please Demeter," Sister Maude confirmed.

Sensing a fish nibbling at his bait, Toby looked to set the hook.

"And now, I am stuck outside the wall with only a few measly coppers to my name, and no way to get back to my mother, who waits for me inside!"

Sister Maude was visibly shaken.

"Well, tuck your head under our wing, little bird, for this flock brings baby cock to mother bird!" Sister Maude boomed.

And so, Toby was draped in holy vestments, handed a censer of burning incense to carry, and welcomed unto the bosom of Demeter.

And when the procession passed the gate, Toby quickly flaked off into the nearest alleyway. One minute there, the next not.

He needed a beer, and a sign had caught his eye. The Busty Wench. Now this seemed promising!

View a video adaptation of this episode of a larger story at https://youtu.be/LblkvonX5m4.

Toby Knotwise, **by Samantha Henze**

14

The Black Eyes of Ulspruth-Dimot

By Lee Clark Zumpe

A misty morning met the awakening village of Madichi. Dawn made pale the cloudy skies, and upon the breeze cascading down from the mountains was a subtle chill. The brooding men and pensive women of the village set about their chores, taking up their labors in the field and in the home and in the market. As the sun rose, limping up into the sky and away from the purple mountains, the mist slipped out of sight and night was at last completely behind them.

This was so, except about the peak of one solitary old crag. Coiled about the summit of this lumbering mass of jagged granite was a peculiar crown of mist, a wispy ring of clouds that seemed to encompass a small haven of darkness.

It was upon this mountain, within this darkness, that dwelled the thing they called Ulspruth-Dimot. No one knew what it was, nor from what infernal lair it had come, nor even how many eons it had nested there upon that peak; but most everyone in the village of Madichi agreed that it was something to be feared.

Few of the villagers that day bothered to greet a company of Iymeridians who came marching through the center of town around mid-morning. Clad in fine armor, with leather breeches and mail shirts, they streamed in off the long road to Ghatlynn and made their way toward the market square. From their sides hung dirks and longswords, and upon their backs were round wooden shields. Some of the red-haired giants carried great battle axes.

There was not a smiling face amongst them. Each and every one appeared grim and withdrawn, their moods somber and serious.

As the solemn procession glided past the homes and pastures and gardens of the villagers, there were some who frowned and some who muttered words beneath their breath and to the ground so that they could not be heard. There were some who shook their heads and some who simply turned away.

Rashybha and Tya beheld the legion as it trudged along.

"Another helping of silage for the Lord Atop the Mountain," said the silver-haired haggard old woman named Rashybha. She was busy tending to a patch of vegetables outside her tiny cottage when she heard the steady tramp of soldiers' boots on the gravel road. Having lived in Madichi for all her years, the old woman had seen the passage of a dozen such armies. "Just another feast for Ulspruth-Dimot."

The other woman, a young maiden named Tya, leaned against a split-rail fence. She admired the handsome lads of the Iymeridian troop as her red locks tossed in the breeze. Upon hearing Rashybha's comments, she grimaced at her elder.

"It's not right," she began, "To speak of them in such a way." She turned toward her neighbor, who was squatting in her modest garden and keeping herself busy. "At least these brave men have the courage to face the Crawling Worm atop that mountain. The men of Madichi shudder at the very mention of that thing, and they cower behind their doors at night and keep their gaze from the mountain as though the mere sight of it could in some way bring to them doom! If only our village possessed the kind of courage that must flow through the blood of these heroes."

"What does courage matter if their crusade is pre-destined to failure?" Rashybha met Tya's gaze and the lines in her forehead deepened. Her empty eyes and pale face spoke of the ageless terror that haunted her always. "Can mere courage succeed where a hundred swords and a thousand warriors pure-of-heart have failed?"

"The death of a courageous soul is far more honorable than the withering demise of a fearful one."

"Death comes to both the valiant and the fearful—why should one hasten it?"

"They risk their lives for you, do you not see that?" The red-haired young woman finally shrugged and turned back toward the Iymeridians. "Without the bravery of soldiers such as these, how can the village hope to survive another winter under the watchful black eyes of Ulspruth-Dimot?"

"You put too much faith in your beaming young lads. Look into their eyes as they shamble by and you will see neither pluck nor mettle; you will see fear, for they know well that death awaits them at the summit of that mountain." The old woman paused and pursed her lips. Tya was a stubborn child, and her resolve was not easily shaken. "You seem to be full of energy and courage," said Rashybha, "Why not join with your noble young soldiers and slay the Crawling Worm atop the accursed mountain?"

Tya had no response to offer Rashybha, but there was no doubt that she had heard the words.

§

The dawn of the following day sent night scattering once more into shadows, and into the deep hollows between the towering mountains surrounding the tiny village of Madichi. The rays of the sun streamed down over the crest of the mountains, bathing the valley with light.

But atop the nearby mountain, upon a broad rock-strewn plateau, a patch of mist refused to dissipate and a pool of darkness scoffed at the rising sun. While in Madichi the farmers tended to their crops and their livestock, and in the market square the shop-keeps took inventory of their stocks and prepared for a day of business, the writhing bodies of a legion of Iymeridians gasped and wept and prayed for the darkness to retreat.

Pitifully, the bloodied soldiers tried drag themselves from the scene of carnage. There were a few dozen of them left, only a handful of the original contingent. Terror and fear mixed in their wide eyes. Masks of desperation clouded their faces.

Merciless flies swirled over a mound of carcasses as a river of steaming, frothy blood streamed from its base. Other corpses, mutilated and unidentifiable, were strewn across the plateau; their chests had been torn open, their organs had spilled to the ground, and their bones had shattered and jutted forth from bluish flesh.

It was onto this scene that a young, red-haired maiden arrived.

Tya picked up a sword from a dead warrior, raised it high in the air, and cried out the name of the cruel god.

"Ulspruth-Dimot! Here is one more mortal body upon which you may feast!" The surviving Iymeridians cringed. They spoke out, trying to silence her, trying to warn her, but she did not hear them. "I offer up this flesh freely, for I know someday you will eat so many mortals your belly will burst open and you too will suffer!"

The Iymeridians, convinced that Tya was either a fool or a lunatic, began to distance themselves from her. She stood firmly, swinging the sword in the air above her head, drawing circles in the darkness.

Soon, the mist began to stir and a cold wind thrashed over the plateau carrying upon its breath a horrid stench. All the wounded Iymeridians could think to do at that moment was scream, and scream they did.

The Grim Morass

By David Samuels

They say you're a paladin, but all I see is a fool.

Look at you: armored like a crawdad with the brains to match. One wrong move on that poleboat and you'll sink to the base of the swamp.

Gimme your hand. Let's get you back on solid ground—if you can call this pier solid. The stilts wobble in the sludge, but nevermind that.

Not a talker, clearly. Don't bother unrolling that scroll. I know all about your oath of silence. Word travels fast among us Marshmen. As the village shaman, I was among the first to learn about your little quest. You seek redemption, yes?

Then go home. Donate gold to war orphans and get on with your life. Truth be told, you'd have better luck floating in that platemail than slaying the Bogroth.

You think you're the first to try? Far from it. That honor belongs to my old master.

It was a generation ago when the Bogroth invaded our lives. Some say it clawed its way out of one of the hells. Others claim that it's the spawn of an ogre and a crocodile. But none can deny its capacity for bloodshed.

Every elder in the village remembers the day of the first slaughter. I was tying herbs to dry in my master's stilthouse when the three surviving fishermen burst inside—three out of twenty.

Blood freckled their faces and dripped down their chattering jaws as they stumbled through their words. Oh, the horrors they'd seen. On and on they ranted about the webbed claws and mawful of fangs that tore their brethren apart.

And yet none of that discouraged my master. Armed with his stave and battle totems, he rowed his canoe into the swamp. You better believe I chased after him. At eighteen cycles, I thought myself invincible. You should've outgrown that by now. What are you, thirty?

Anyway, my master forced me to turn back. He also had me promise to protect the village in his absence. So I returned to our stilthouse and saw to the wounded while waiting for him to return.

Return he did—one piece at a time. His bloated limbs floated downriver the next morning, tattooed flesh bobbing against a neighboring houseboat. Hardly enough left of him to embalm in his funerary cocoon.

Still think you have what it takes?

Hrmph. The set of your jaw tells me all I need to know.

I was once like you, brimming with hope. The Bogroth put an end to that. It was a lesson I learned firsthand.

That helmet doesn't hide your rising brows, you know.

You're curious. Who wouldn't be? I'm one of the few who's encountered the monstrosity and lived to tell the tale.

If those brows go any higher, they'll knock off your helmet.

Alright, I'll humor you. For a price. Don't give me that look. We're desperate, not greedy. Hardly any traders venture here anymore, for obvious reasons. So how about loosening the strings of that pouch by your hip?

Fifteen measly cherubim? Fine. Wipe your feet before you come inside. I don't need those boots tracking sludge over my reeds. Don't mind the smoke in here—sandalwood keeps dark spirits at bay.

Here, drink this.

What? Never seen a bowl of tea before? Typical Flaurian. If you spent less time crusading against other cultures and more time learning from them, you might look less befuddled. Now, drink.

Ah, nothing like that minty aroma to clear the sinuses.

Where was I….Right. After my master met his fate, I was heartbroken. How could he be dead when his bed was still unmade from that morning? When his Jakim cards were still strewn across our table, midway through a round?

In my grief, I swore to exact vengeance on the Bogroth. But I'd also promised my master that I'd protect the people on his behalf. If I lost my life, our town would be *akriipii*: cursed as shamanless. Better to bide my time for my chance at revenge.

That chance coasted into the village five years later. The sleek red oarship belonged to an expedition from the Penny Cantons, headed by a perfumist by the name of Kienne. I remember because he referred to himself in the third person—an insufferable habit.

Awfully sure of himself, too. Anyone would be, with a band of Veldtian mercenaries in tow. By that grimace, I'm guessing you don't care for Veldtians.

Ah, but of course! You must've fought them in your crusade against the Penny Cantons. These lands bore the brunt of that particular war, mind you. And you can call the Pencelings heretics all you like, but you must admit they choose their sellswords wisely.

All armored in suits of lacquered chitin, the dozen mercenaries waited aboard the ship while Kienne strutted into my stilthouse without so much as an invitation.

I was carving a fertility totem at the time. Annoyed by the interruption, I was about to insult his mother for failing to teach him manners when he explained the reason behind his visit. He'd amassed a fortune distilling colognes from crocodile musk, you see, and believed he could reap greater profits with the odor from the Bogroth's glands. All he needed was someone to navigate the ever-shifting waters, and did I have anyone in mind?

I volunteered my services on the spot. Here was the chance I'd been waiting for so long. With our forces combined, nothing could stop us.

Such is the folly of youth.

From the foredeck of the vessel, I led us upriver amid the swish of oars and croak of bullfrogs. The ship wasn't built for these waters, so the cabin sometimes tore away tresses of ivy. More than once we had to disembark and shove the stern across mudbanks and banyan roots. But none of that fazed the Veldtians nearly as much as what they beheld that night.

To be honest, I was surprised they spotted it by the dim paper lanterns that dangled from our railposts.

A row of stakes jutted from the water, and, impaled upon those stakes, well….

Several mercenaries seized their prayer beads in terror. You wouldn't think it from their bulky frames, but the Veldtians are close cousins to Marshmen. We roamed the savannahs long before the Deluge swept in, so we share a similar language today. Hence why I understood fragments of their speech when they claimed the waters to be cursed.

"What you see is no curse," I told them, "but desperation."

In the hopes of appeasing the Bogroth, a few hotheads had raided our funerary cocoons for bodies to impale on the outskirts of the village. As if those fetid corpses could satisfy what warm flesh could not. Patches of skin had sloughed off their faces, revealing nasal sockets as dark as their pecked-out eyeholes.

It wouldn't be long until the villagers grew bolder. All the more reason to put an end to this nightmare before it consumed us in both body and soul.

Despite my words, the Veldtians remained shaken. They believed impalement to be the foulest form of mutilation. It chained the deceased to this world, damning them to roam Euvael as vengeful wraiths.

Indeed, it felt as if unquiet spirits haunted us all through the night. Silver eyes glinted from the shadowy riverbanks while unseen beastlings screeched over treetops.

How is that tea, by the way? Good, good.

It wasn't the discord of the night that we had to fear, but the quiet instead. Very soon, an oppressive silence fell upon us; a loaded hush that warned us to turn back, for no prey dared roam these waters except the Veldtians and their foolhardy captain.

Me? Why, I was the predator.

As were my twenty brethren who burst from the bulrushes. Blowguns in hand, they shot darts into the gaps between the Veldtians' chitin plates. Not just any darts, but ones dipped in toxins.

Similar to what you drank.

Yours is slower-acting, of course. You should be feeling it about now. Somewhat woozy, yes? Go ahead and reach for that sword if you like.

Hah! See? You can scarcely lift it.

While you're still conscious, I'll let you in on a secret. There's no such thing as the Bogroth. Those impaled bodies were sacrifices, yes, but to a god beyond your ken. There are hundreds of other corpses visible by daylight. Good thing I navigated those fools under the sister moons.

Why, you ask? Because rumor of the Bogroth lures your ilk here. I can think of no better sacrifice than the knights and mercenaries who've used these fens as their battleground while my people suffer the consequences. Simply put, *you* are the Bogroth.

Shush, now.

Master is coming.

Poseidon **by Mark Rhodes-Taylor**

Emhain Ablach

By Joshua S. Fullman

A slate horizon keeps captive none
who'd gaze with eyes eternal,
but the merciless wind on a lurid sea
snuffs bonfires into used tallows
and crushes the voyager wan.

He sits, a king in his armchair,
lit in the frozen light of spring's first dawn,
watching static waves rage listless.
Hungry, he stirs gingerly the stone tor,
seeking a white sail in the window
to light the perpetual mist,
spreading his mind in every crevice
for an undiscovered pin.

                  And still
the feathered bed seduces him,
the cankered sword weightless on his fleece,
the ache of content vibrating
through every breath and hollow.

       Her footsteps on the stairs a dial,
she strides within without a courteous knock,
her long locks reminiscent of a woman
he knew well but none too true.
She raises from among her armaments
a bowl of dried apples and a smile.

       What sorrows weigh on such a morn,
she asks, and offers him a tray,
ignoring the ambivalent shrug
of his hand.
                Grief cannot be your store
in such a seat, where star
and ocean dance, where dreams
awake on tapestries, where nature
tailors to a woman's touch.
You'd trade not these changeless days
for Glastonia's treacherous tarns,
nor would its icy meres forgive your faults
nor heal your hurts—
which someday soon shall heal.
Remember how we three bore you,
love and honor befit your rank,
apportioning our hospitality
in this lavish citadel.
              Why bind
yourself, dear brother, with filaments
of happiness beyond?

Too broken, she, you won't recall,
too sod with sad disloyalty;
true, penitent he, yet still he harbors
in desire, would break all earthly vows
of court or priest to drink the tempest.
The world has also since moved on:
few out there peer through broken frames
and ancient books, too filled
with dread of purpose to pray
for your return.
                              Retire, my lord,
take your delight of ease,
for though we'd cling to glassy ocean rocks
the withered fig of men cannot repair
the mortal wound.
Take breakfast, let us break
these daily walks on empty parapets
and hermetical debates.
Leave glory now to younger men.
who, unwise and inexperienced,
yet still must test their strength
upon the ruin of the earth.
Raise not your dread of plague
and inquisition, of bloodshed, bureaucrat
and atom; such days must come
in despite of the throne.
And if the crown still perched your brow
would not the mob resent your table?
Or does the cocked eyebrow quick forget
a hobbled commonwealth,
with its name and scepter
spread across a burning continent?
The tattered scroll of history is raped
by idealists and diabolists alike—
and so alike they whisper.
                              Come, earth holds no wonder for the spirit.
Shall we recline and heal this grievous hurt
and let the meal work. A worried mind
shall never soothe. I'll even sheathe
that blade for you and leave it till some morrow—
the day, I'm sure, not distant far,
when you'll take up your armor and return.

        The king receives her gifts, lays no response
to words worn true by use. She slips away,
he munches apples, no cup to cleanse his palate,
and every bite a phantasy
of a court, a sage, and brothers,
the picture of a girl astride a bed—
his dream his heaven's horror,
and he a rusted lyre with golden, broken strings.
Eyes weakening, he rubs his temple, tries
to spy a sail, and shuffles to his bed,
straining to hear the trumpet of the deep.

The Little Wild

By Julian Grant

The "Little Wild" is what she called it—and it shall be ours forever.

We had bought the farmhouse when we finally had had enough of the city (Poppy agreed, the city had become too dangerous and noisy). As we were both older, without children, having met later in life at the Popular Culture Association Conference in Boston, we were both determined to make our soon encroaching Senior years as enjoyable as possible. We made for an unlikely couple what with Poppy's paper on psychoanalytic theory and gender in Fairy Tales, while my own talk was a stump speech for the Graduate Program in library science we offered at Northwestern. We bonded on archival methods, preservation, organization, and best practices, marrying almost a year to the date of our first encounter. No odder couple had there perhaps ever been. We were visually unique as well. She, Rubenesque and committed to smoking a pack a day, while I maintained the thin physique that I had championed while at school. Poppy would tease me as "*Jack Sprat, the boy who would eat no fat*" nursery rhyme hero, and I was too polite to ever voice her comparison.

We were both in our late forties when we finally moved to the country and bought the large old farmhouse that had been abandoned by its previous owners and which needed some work before it could be occupied. The house was a mess of disrepair and neglect, but Poppy was determined to make it into something beautiful. She took on the restoration project with gusto while I busied myself at my job as a senior archivist at Northwestern University Library's Special Collections Department. I had worked there since graduating from university (the same one where Poppy studied, it turned out), having spent several years working on my master catalog of the variant manuscripts and publications of George MacDonald. His "Golden Key" was the basis of my theory to the Princesses, Giants, and Fae who gamboled through his writings.

Together, in our new home, we both worked diligently to put everything to order. I sanded, plugged, and painted inside while Poppy took on the front garden. We both agreed that the garden acreage in the back of the house was best left as is. Originally the farm had boasted a small greens and herbs bounty that had exploded into a warren of wild, overlapping vegetation. Thick snarls of basil, celery, and lettuce we were stumped to identify (I found it finally—flashy trout back) had swallowed the full garden, with a thick entangled row of white ash soaring above us at the edge of the property. All of the original farmland had been sold off and developed into housing plots that loomed around us and the area we now called "The Little Wild."

I spent a lot of time out there, sitting on the back porch facing the overgrown garden looking up at the night sky. The air was so clear here that I could see all of the stars each evening.

"You're not afraid to be alone out here?" Poppy asked one night as she joined me by my side. "I mean, you don't feel like you need someone else around." She put her hand on mine where it rested on my knee and squeezed gently. "It's okay if you are," she said softly, but firmly.

"No," I replied.

Unlike Poppy, I saw no gossamer strands of mystery here nor anything to worry about. I was content living in our idyllic home with Poppy by my side and had no fear of the unknown or metaphysical wonders at work in the dark. Here, in the peace of our home, I could ponder the play and nonsense of MacDonald's work as I rejoiced in the peace and quiet. Poppy's study, in the spare bedroom upstairs, was where she wrote and dreamed and lived with the myriad of creatures that made up her life's work. As a bibliophile, all I needed were my books and the serenity of our farm. Wrapped in a blanket on the back porch, I graded papers, and Polly would slip out to smoke, having agreed that cigarettes inside was a to-be-avoided decision. I abandoned my study of syntax, language, and idiom as I turned to her.

"Look, there are fireflies," Poppy cried as she snapped off the small reading lamp we had set up for my work. Instantly, we were transported into the thick dark you only find outside of the city. As a formerly dedicated urban creature, I had fibbed to Poppy when I told her earlier that I was not afraid to sit alone in the dark in "The Little Wild." Being fully alone in the dark was something I did not relish—but I knew that my fears were irrational. The little tests I would set for myself to push beyond my natural reservations were long ingrained. It would not serve my wife to know how my heart started to race, the spit souring in my mouth as the velvet crush of night consumed us.

The flitter-fly of the insects coasted above and beyond the snarls of brambles and vegetables. In the dark, I reached for my wife's hand, wiping mine first on the blanket as I willed my heart to stop its pounding. We sat there, neither of us speaking, as Polly sighed, her cigarette forgotten.

The next thing I knew, the fireflies were gone and I was alone on the couch in the dark. "Poppy?" I whispered, glancing about myself as I wiped the sleep from my crusted eyes. "Poppy?" I whispered again, my voice hoarse as I sat up and looked about the garden for her. There was no sign of her anywhere in the backyard. I stood from the couch and made my way up to our bedroom, where she might already be abed. It wasn't uncommon for me to doze outside only to find her already asleep.

She was not there either—nor were any of her clothes or belongings strewn about on the floor as they had been when we returned home after dinner with friends a few hours earlier. The empty rooms sent me into a panic; it felt like I had awoken, like Rip Van Winkle, only to find the world had changed alarmingly.

I glanced outside towards "The Little Wild" as a light, amber-colored, spilled from deep within the snare of shadowed greenery. Peering outside the window, I could see pockets of illumination sparking to life in the black night. "Why would she go back there?" I wondered as I slipped back downstairs, grasping the flashlight by the back door.

Stepping out into the now cold very early morning, I tried to turn the light on only to realize that the batteries were not working.

"Polly?!" I cried, a little louder now, concerned that she might be back there with a little candle or match. She would have surely taken the flashlight to find her way—and if she too discovered that it wasn't working, perhaps she was finding her way by candlelight?

Underneath my feet, the ground was slick, showing the clear track of what I could only assume was Polly moving deep into the "Wild." I rubbed at my face, pushing the last of sleep away as I saw two, three amber lights pop to life in the garden. There, deep in the brickle, flickering lights too big to be fireflies sparkled as the tantalizing aroma of roasting meats tickled my nose.

I pushed further into the weeds, inwardly cursing myself for not thinning the stalks and strands of wild weeds and bushes that created the maze that was our back garden. Polly had loved how rich and untamed the world was—"...a home for small animals and perhaps more," she'd teased one night as I nodded in half-agreement.

As I pushed further into the bush, I recited to myself the various eponymous fairytales and legends I knew that had influenced Irving's classic tale. The third-century story of the legendary sage, Epimenides of Knossos, the Christian story of the Seven Sleepers, and the German folktale "Peter Klaus" all boasted elements of the rudely awakened sleeper finding the world changed much to their shock and dismay. My own revelation was surely more prosaic, and I would soon find my wife curled up reading or perhaps writing by candlelight. I had long learned to tolerate the eccentricities of our marriage and Poppy's whims, as she had endured my endless and systematic organization.

"It is what makes us special," Poppy had smiled, one night when we were in bed talking, as couples do, of the faults and findings of their marriage. "I dream, you do, too, and together we shine," she said, snuggling next to me.

I crouched down as a robust wild rosebush blocked my path, the lights of the golden yellow candles just beyond.

"Did you bring food out here?" I called as, again, the scent of rich-seasoned meat came to my attention. She'd brought home the remnants of the prime rib she had out tonight and perhaps she had fancied a late-night, early morning snack as she explored the garden. Again, another eccentricity one learns to live with when married. Poppy enjoyed her food.

"I'm not hungry," I called out. "But I'll bring out some wine if you'd like?"

As Poppy was the one who had chosen this spot for our impromptu rendezvous, it seemed fitting that we should enjoy ourselves. She would be happy to see me, and I could only hope that tonight would be like all other nights when we were together: uneventful and peaceful. The night air was warm and heavy with the scent of the wildflowers in bloom from "The Little Wild" as I struggled through into the other side.

"Shall I get the wine then?"

I pushed myself through the small gap in the foliage, marveling at how my larger-than-me wife could have navigated such tight quarters. As I pushed through the final cover, my eyes popped wide as I beheld the miniature fantasy world before me.

There, under four stanchions burning bright, my wife danced in abandon with the sprites and fairies I had read about throughout my life but never believed in. A pig, impossibly small, roasted on a spit turned by leaf-clad people all clapping and singing as Poppy gamboled and played with them.

You must understand, fables, myths, and fairytales may have been my area of study—but like most academics dedicated to any discipline, I had long lost the fancy and marvel that made the tales special. My world was one of order, versioning, and cataloging. Poppy was the true believer while I was the skeptic. I no sooner believed in the world of fairy than I did the modern-day equivalents of Bigfoot or Elvis or other celebrities still alive after death. None of this made any sense to me.

Yet, there, right in front of me, my wife danced in miniature and smiled and laughed as the assembled peoples celebrated her. None paid any mind to me at all, impossibly large, as I watched the joyous celebration unfold. I could barely breathe as the dance continued unabated.

"How are you doing this?" I called out. "This isn't possible." She looked at me finally, smiling as she danced, and called out, "I will always love you."

The crowd cheered louder than ever as Poppy continued her dance with the sprites and fairies. She smiled at me again, that beautiful smile of hers which always made my thrilled heart ache.

And then I woke, on the couch on the back patio as the sun blossomed across the sky. It was now morning and I had spent the night outside, apparently.

I laughed, hardly able to contain myself, as I gathered up my papers and books, none the worse for wear for having spent the night outdoors, looking forward to sharing with Polly my own Winkle story. Orkney's tale of the Ring of Brodgar immediately came to mind as well, as did H.G. Wells's *The Sleeper Awakes* as I clambered up the stairs. I was now Zelazny's science-fiction protagonist Corwyn, having survived the underground lair with otherworldly people. Poppy would adore this.

The doctor says it was the combination of early menopause, her BMI, and the cigarettes that caused the heart failure. She'd died sometime earlier, while I was sleeping on the couch outside. He assured me that she hadn't felt any pain.

I had been a very lucky man. I was forty-eight years old, and Poppy was forty-nine when she passed. Each night she dances still in "The Little Wild," and if I am careful and the time is right, I am able to go and see her in the wee midnight hours. I have a lot of work to do still. I have to write the story that Poppy always wanted me to write, and then publish it as a final gift. It will be an epic tale about two people who are both immortal and whose love endures. It will begin as all good fairy tales begin.

Once upon a time...

Clover for Archivists by **Phillip Fitzsimmons**

A Poem by Joe R. Christopher

C. S. Lewis's Meditation over "The Book of the Leoun"

One wonders what did Chaucer mean to make?
A version out of French, for versing's sake?

A bit of praise Prince Lionel to flatter,
Upon his wedding, with other praise to scatter?

Or neither these—a tossed-off bagatelle
To fill an idle hour with idler spell?

But no! not that! the king of every beast
Was surely called to roar at nobler feast.

The lion of the tribe of Judah's praised
For breaking seals, which angels all amazed.

But that's not Chaucer's style, nor choice of vision—
Except, at times, the Parson's—by decision.

And yet, a diff'rent role—still Leonine—
Would somehow fit, would with my thought align.

But not like Spenser's lion, whom Una saved—
Not quite, not quite, despite some foes outbraved.

For then Sansloy, the lion did defeat,
And pierced its heart by sword, to win their meet.

So not as Spenser wrote in his great tale—
No sword when met, the lion to impale.

But still, romance is right to entertain:
The lion could both die and rise again.

Talking Things over in Hospital

By S. Dorman

Oh, bother this, thought Jack Lewis with but a small portion of his mind. He was taken up just now with bigger things, being squandered on an enormous pain radiating from his center up into his neck and jaw; pain like lightning along his arms, through to his back, and down into his gut. He was pouring sweat and could not breathe. And they had taken hold of his arms, two strong men apparently, and were laying him out. *But I was going to Ireland today*, he thought.

Then he seemed to be coming out of it as though leaving behind tendrils of pain and drawing back into his core, his being no longer radiating a massive thrombosis. He could feel the great pain unleashing him... a bit more.... There. It was gone. Eyes still closed, he thought about sitting up. He smelled smoke. A nurse—it must've been—said with prompt irritation, "Who is smoking? There is no smoking in here! You will send us sky-high!"

There was silence. After a bit he opened his eyes and looked about in the dark. Yes, someone was smoking, though the nurse was apparently gone. The smoker stood there against the open window, backlit by the moon. Haloed, especially his silvery hair. Whoever it was did not so much block the moon's light as give it a certain form. As though the man in it, meaning the shadow upon its bright face, had come down to stand in Lewis's room, its brightness yet surrounding him. Lewis moved his head a bit and saw the great disc shining beyond the light-limned dark form. But again now both were clouded with prodigious puffs of smoke.

Oh, bother this, he thought. But, surprised, he smiled a bit and said in his highly cultured voice, "Hullo! haven't seen you in a while." Surely it was Mark Twain on one of his inconvenient visits again. "Been some time since." He thought, I was *happy* ...very happily married to Joy and working on the Queen of Glome's book.

The man-in-the-moon turned, and the moonlight fell directly across his white front. And Lewis saw it was so. Mark Twain was dressed in his habitual white serge suit, his shaggy hair gleaming, his gaze glimmering on his friend in a not unfriendly but decidedly considering fashion. He said something in a low voice from beneath his brush of a mustache, something that Lewis, lying there, scarcely heard.

"What's that?" Lewis said. "I-beg-your-pardon?"

"I said, 'I think you are dead.' "

Jack Lewis sat up. He said, "Preposterous. And, anyway, the only time you come is when I am dreaming." He had swung his legs over the edge of the hospital bed. He was wearing only a hospital gown. It felt drafty but he did not want to ask for the lattice closed now nor go past his friend to do it himself. He liked fresh air—moon-shining air, he thought it. He sat there a moment, feet and legs a-dangle.

"Is that so?" asked Twain, the midwestern twang of his American accent gentled just a bit by a soft southern quality.

"What do you mean? Of course, I was dreaming—How else could those visitations and conversations have occurred? —I mean, I *am* dreaming. *You* are the one who is dead. I'll wake up soon and go to Ireland with Douglas and meet Warnie. In the meantime, what do you want?"

"Oh, now," said the other with a slight smile. He drew a moment on his cigar. "Is that any way to start a conversation after all this time, 'What do you want?' Especially as profound a

35

conversation as we are about to have?" The smoke drifted out the opening, reflecting a moment off the divided panes in the casement at an oblique angle to the open windowsill.

The bags under his brown eyes apiece with his somewhat pudgy face, Lewis gazed at him, resisting the impulse to rub both face and eyes in hope of dispelling the apparition.

"Well, Clemens, or Mark Twain, or the Mysterious Stranger or whoever it is, if I were dead!..." He stopped. "Firstly, if I remember my catechism, I would not be seeing— ...and I would be *like*— well. I would be seeing the One I'm to be like when I pass from this body and world. Right now I am decidedly *not like* that One. —And secondly, distinctly, *you* do not look a'tall like Him." He tried eyeing the other pointedly, then gave it up. He gazed at him. "Say something," he said.

But the other seemed in no hurry, just stood, quietly smoking his cigar in the moonlight and looking at Jack Lewis. "Well," he said at last, "maybe you are only sort of dead."

"Sort of! *Sort* of dead?!"

He had got off the bed and come near Twain in the moonlight. Perhaps he thought of testing this... this... this situation by reaching out to touch him. But Samuel Clemens stood back just a bit, as though in subtle warning. And Lewis, ever polite, took the hint and stood still. Instead, he gazed out onto the moonlit surface of treetops, just past the car park, thinking.

Clemens made a small gesture with his lit cigar, its tip redly glowing, and Lewis turned back to see what was pointed to. He stood stock still. "What's that?" he said.

There in his bed a man was lying. It was the oddest thing.... How could there be a man in the bed he'd only just vacated? But another odd thing: The man was slightly reclining, and his head was shrouded in, in.... "What is that?" he said again. But he was thinking, I'm not really capable of such dreams... *unless... inspired...?* The man's head was transparently veiled, in some sort of plastic cylinder with pointy top (somehow Lewis's own head, he saw). A long slim flexible tube was attached to the veil's top. From a tank nearby. Yes, he knew now what it was.

"An oxygen tent, it's called," said Twain.

"Of course. Is he dead?" asked Lewis.

"That's what I think," said the other. "Sort of."

How odd. That is me? That is me.

"Your hands were clasped across your middle a moment ago. But now, you see, they are fallen away at your sides. They could not hold together after you left."

Lewis went near and gazed at the man—at himself. "But," he could not take away his gaze. "Why am I out—here? *What* am I, then? He felt strange, he felt queer looking at himself lying there. And...he felt a simple unwonted fondness for the creature.

"Well, I don't know. A sort of gas, I guess."

"Sort— sort! What do you mean by that word? Define it. Define your use of *sort* for me." He looked at Twain and then back at the man again. "Either I am a gas or I am not."

"Ah," said Mark Twain. "Your old master comes to aid you, the logical one, the rational— what was his name—who gave your mind its rigorous training? The 'Great Knock', he was?"

"William T. Kirkpatrick," said Lewis crisply. "And gas cannot speak."

"How do you know?"

"Because I've never heard—." But he stopped, gazing still at the man in the oxygen tent. That was no good. Never having heard of it does not make a thing impossible. "It has no mechanism, no medium whereby.... —This is preposterous."

Twain drew on his cigar, its ash glowing very brightly now, a spot of orange reflecting off the plastic veil. He said, "Why not check yourself for gas?"

Lewis turned away from himself to stare back at Twain. Then he gazed again on the man in the bed and moved nearer. Jack Lewis, it seemed, lay there in the moonlight, inert. He did not need to check it for gas, did not bend near for that, because somehow he knew. But he leaned over himself anyway. He wanted to experience this, this strange thing of spreading oneself, one's attention, over one's form. In this hovering he did indeed confirm that there was very little gas, if any, in him. He said, "I don't think he's quite... quite... breathing."

"You mean he's sort of not breathing? Or he sort of is."

Now Lewis stood back off himself and glanced sharply at Clemens. "Aren't you—weren't you *younger* the last time I saw you? A lot younger? Where is your younger version? He was somehow kinder." Samuel Clemens seemed, as ever, too able to touch upon his irascibility, as though pulling levers or pushing buttons.

There was silence as Clemens looked at him. The silence lengthened. The silence grew distinct, profound. As Lewis gazed toward the moonlit Twain unmoving, the silence itself seemed somehow moving, swelling; somehow as though a breath he could not feel was slowly clearing away the smoke and sending it out the open window. But then, rapidly, a change overtook the straight white old man standing before him in the moonlight. A transformation gathering his frame into the compact likeness of a child, smoothing its body smaller, fresher, crisper; his wrinkled shaggy features swiftly modeling, in vivid brightness, extravagance of relish and joy. Boyishly elastic, a bright high laughter shot out his mouth, his red hair shining above the face of his childish glee. But, swiftly then, he lengthened out, standing a straight old whitened man again. And somehow the cigar was back in his hand, though Lewis was quite certain he'd not had it in the state of a child (now gone). It happened so quickly and so completely. Jack Lewis was stunned by this transfiguring power.

Oh no, he thought, *I am not capable of dreaming that. In no way capable.*

And he was weeping. Weeping.

"There, there," said Twain. He seemed at a lost, just a little. "Perhaps I should not—."

"Oh, don't you see?! Oh, *don't* you?! Why couldn't it be Joy? *Joy!*" It came out with vehemence. But he had to stop this violence. He turned away and wiped his eyes.

Clemens looked down, sorry. Then he whispered, "No, I guess you're not so dead after all." And more softly still, considering, "...Some of you is still left in there."

He raised his moon-shining head.

SunMoon by **Phillip Fitzsimmons**

A Poem by David Sparenberg

Amergin*

Heart of the deer
to a human heart.
Eye of the deer
to a human eye.
Song of the deer
to a human voice.
Dance of the deer
to human feet;
to limbs and sinews and feet.
And to the soul of beauty
as a woman knows it
And to the soul of beauty
as a man may learn.
Heart of the stone
to human tenacity
to gravity and strength.
Memory of the stone
to human dreaming.
Story of the stone
in a field, on a road, submerged in a stream
story of stone
to the human sojourn.
And the chant of stone
to a human poem.
To vision and rhyme and rhythm of drum:
to sounding of the drum of the human soul.

Heart of the tree
to human courage.
Roots of the tree

to longevity.
To depths and the heights
that a seed can become. Branches
of tree
to human prayer.
Leaves of tree
to the seasons of love:
to the breath and sighs
and the tears and whispers.
And to the harp of human longing.

Heart of the dolphin
to a human heart.
Song of the dolphin
to mortal ecstasy.
Play of the dolphins
to human joy.
And the enchantment of dolphins
to human magic and melody.
To those, lucky, who are chosen
by waves and whales and reefs and sandy shore.
And by the depths of pipes of the ocean:
the fiddles and pipes of the ocean.

Heart
of the mist of time
to the human mind.
Heart
of the moon
to the human heart.
Heart of the sun
to the human soul.

Amergin: the legendary first poet of Ireland

Vargar by Yiming Zhao

Vargar
Story by Andoni Cossio
Image by Yiming Zhao

An earlier version of this work won the XI International University Short Story Contest in English language in Honor of "Félix Menchacatorre" (2020), organized by the University of the Basque Country (UPV/EHU) and the University Study Abroad Consortium (USAC).

Squinting my eyes and resuming the frenzied spurring, I headed unflinchingly towards the setting sun. The gap between my steed and the couple of pursuers was widening, we were almost outside their shooting range. But suddenly I found myself flying and shielding the wolf cubs as I could from the imminent fall. I turned around and saw horrified my prostrate horse pierced by two arrows, barely enduring the pangs of pain. They were coming.

Wolf den raids in search of cubs, infrequent until that spring, had been merciless. These animals, no longer slain for their pelts or in self-defense, found themselves in peril of being wiped out. Associating wolves with witchcraft, the demented villagers had burnt fellow women and their offspring suspicious of being in league with the lupine creatures. I escaped but had nowhere to go. Mother wolves raise others' young when their own have perished. I wished to partake in the same noble action of helping those who still had descendants left. I owed them much as they had never harmed you, daddy, or our cattle—the reason behind the whistleblowing.

The two men dismounted and approached me. The cubs could not flee; with the membranes covering their undeveloped eyes, they were as blind as bats. One of the pursuers had his bow at the ready, the other drew a dagger. My heart throbbed as the cold blade got closer to my throat. Yet I knew we were not alone.

The men found themselves prey to dozens of stealthy wolf mothers wishing to take revenge on the brutes for the cub massacre. Tears filled my eyes; I closed them and prayed. When silence reigned in the woodlands once again it was dark, and I could only see the lamp-like glow of the wolves' eyes. I freed the cubs, who clumsily sniffed their way to their mothers. The pack started retreating into the forest, occasionally stopping and casting inviting glances. Our kindred had abandoned us; thus I resolved to join theirs.

As you know, my child, *vargr* means either wolf or outlaw.

We are both now.

Vargr is a real Old Norse strong singular noun (pl. *Vargar*) and stems from the reconstructed Proto-Germanic **Uargaz*. *Vargr* is cognate with the Old English *wearh*, Old High German *warg* and Old Saxon *uuarag*. I have particularly chosen the Old Norse term in order to vaguely set the short story around a given historical time and at an approximate unspecified location. The masculine noun *Vargr* is in its second sense only seemingly applicable to adult men who were ousted from their respective societies and had to live in the wild (and hence its association with the first meaning "wolf"). However, I have conceived a mythical setting in which both senses are applicable to a woman (and her child), and that re-interprets this pejorative word in a new more positive light, hinting that the change of status hereby leads to a new beginning. For more information on the noun *vargr* see Robinson, Fred C. "Germanic *Uargaz (OE Wearh) and the Finnish Evidence." *Inside Old English: Essays in Honour of Bruce Mitchell*, edited by John Walmsley, paperback ed., Chichester: Wiley Publishers, 2016, pp. 242-267.

Bibliography

Robinson, Fred C. "Germanic *Uargaz (OE Wearh) and the Finnish Evidence." In *Inside Old English: Essays in Honour of Bruce Mitchell*, edited by John Walmsley, Chichester: Wiley Publishers, 2016, pp. 242-67.

Peredur in the Wasteland

By Joe R. Christopher

When Peredur, unknighted yet,
rode out on questing, one vignette,
more than all his adventures else,
left mental scars and psychic welts.
Ah, strange it was, and most obscure—
a parable sans meaning sure.

    For while he rode, the forest green
turned dry and brown, all unforeseen;
the leaves were fallen, branches bare,
though shone the sun through springtime's air.
The birds were stilled—most like, they'd flown
to greener lands with flowers strewn.
No squirrels chattered from the trees,
as if the spring had ta'en disease.

    At last, the barren trees were ended:
a barren valley 'fore him descended.
He paused and let his gelding graze
on the dry grass; the strange malaise
spread down the vale before his eyes—
all brown, all gray, no greensome dyes.
Far off, on a main road, there went
a caravan, on leaving bent,
with wagons, folks afoot, horseback;
and dust rose up along its track.

    When Peredur rode on, he saw
a dusty field with a dusty plow,
a man and bone-thin horse; in need,
in drifty furrows the man sowed seed.
But where was rain, that lucky chance,
to raise the germinated lance?
Where was the green and wholesome wheat,
or where the barley, with grains replete?

    Later, he spied a lake or sea:
sun-glinted waves flash normally;
but as he approached, the creeks were dry
which would have fed, and would liquefy,
the body in the valley lying.
He feared the sea-let might be dying.
He found the beach with markings lined,
as the water had dropped, increasingly brined;
no doubt an outlet, which'd kept this fresh,
was now too high to hydromesh.

The shoreward waves, blown by the breeze,
were slimed and stank with obsequies.

    And there, beside the stagnant sea,
that lowered lake, upon a quay,
surrounded by his courtiers tall,
a king or lord or prince of all,
an earl or duke—his title no guessing—
on a cushioned seat, sat there a-fishing.
And as he sat, he sang, in lore,
of fragile ruins on the shore.

    This duke was dressed in robes of blue,
but dusty robes all through and through.
No crown or coronet he wore—
his brow a band of silver bore;
no precious stones were set thereon,
no rubies, diamonds, carnelian,
but graven was upon the front
an ichthus, like on many a font.
But stranger still, so Per'dur thought,
was what this lord elsewhere had got:
a white codpiece at first it was,
then seen as whitesome bandages.

    When Peredur drew near and came
upon the quay, he saw the aim
had gained no catch: all fishless he,
who sought there piscatorially.
"Why drop your line in those dead waters?
Why cast in that with stagnant attars?"

    The prince replied with sudden ire,
"Stranger, until you shall retire,
to bed and board, within our castle,
ask not such foolish quids and facile!
I tell you now: 'Mind your own purpose!
Ask not, from your stupidity's surplus—
until tonight, you're not our guest!'"
He jerked his hook, by dead weeds possessed.

    Per'dur's hand on his sword had
tightened;
but then he saw that, and felt enlightened,
the king, all damaged in his crotch,
had blood there soaking through, a swatch.
His genitalia wounded, surely;

42

the pain his temper shaping poorly.
No verbal reply was there avowed,
for Per'dur pitied him, and bowed.

But that had ended, so it seemed,
the fishing in the slime unteemed;
eight courtiers raised up high their lord,
his litter raised with one accord,
and shouldered him who could not walk,
carrying him with little shock.
As the procession wound away,
Peredur saw his horse astray—
one of the courtiers had its bridle
and led it peacefully in his idyll;
another gestured, "Join in with us."
In silence went the courteous.
Perhaps in honor, thought Peredur,
no one goes faster than the earl.

Beyond a grove of barren trees,
upon a hillock, by degrees,
the courtiers and the litter went—
to where, with strange accoutrement,
the walled estate was highly placed.
The stones with old designs were traced;
A barbican beside the gate
Had spiral carvings foliolate;
The keystone of the gateway arch,
'neath which did litter-bearers march,
was cut to show an ichthus fair
(but who was fishing for it there?).
Inside, a maze of buildings stood,
stone-walled and strong, thick-beamed in wood.

But as they entered, their silence broke;
to Peredur his neighbors spoke,
welcoming him. And then the prince,
his litter lowered, did lightly evince
his courtesy and his courtliness—
"Hail, O stranger, may you God bless,
for deigning, despite death's dryness drear,
to come to dine and dream with us here.
All that we have, though poor, is yours;
wee welcome, despite the discomfitures.
Our kingdom is weak, as you have seen;
but you enrich our dried terrene,
like gentle rain upon the soil,
engendering crops, which welcome toil
will harvest later, giving food
with all its widest amplitude.
Welcome again, though we don't rise,

having our wounds: we agonize
that we can't greet you firmly now,
with clasp instead of words, we vow,
for words are weak to show our love,
most like an empty, unhanded glove;
as is, we can but say anew,
with thorough meaning: Thrice welcome, you."

And Peredur, now knowing his rank,
dropped on a knee and said his thanks.
"O noble lord, O gentle king,
your speech is too beflattering—
I'm not worthy of your high praise,
and cannot match you phrase for phrase,
at all: but this, at least, I say:
the honor's mine as your guest today."

The king then gestured him to rise,
and soon the king, in a different guise,
was raised—and carried on a chair
elsewhere in the buildings there,
while Per'dur, given a fair room
and unguents, no water, with which to groom,
prepared himself to feast that night—
after the drought, with an appetite.
Indeed, the household well prepared
to feed the hungry courtiers yared;
although the food was mostly imported,
nevertheless, it was nicely assorted:
smoked meats and salted meats were served;
dried fruits, and turnips well preserved,
brought layered in straw; unleaved bread;
old wine from cellars—on these they fed.

With tables trestle-raised and seating,
within the hall, before the eating,
saw Peredur the kingdom's queen,
dressed all in palest aquamarine;
her brow by narrow silver band,
with ichthus 'graved, was neatly spanned—
a slender woman and middle aged,
but dark-haired still, as Per'dur gauged;
she laughed and kept a flow of chatter
which seemed to have but little matter—
her hands were seldom still, at peace,
but fluttered with a fine caprice,
touching now this, now that, in fine,
or trembling as they raised some wine;
he noted, with a vague surprise,
dark circles lay beneath her eyes.
She greeted her guest with words fair spoken,

bidding him welcome, with truth unbroken;
she said in addition, "I hope you'll ask
if I can do the smallest task;
or if you find our customs odd,
do not you fear I'll think you prod—
but ask, and I'll explain them all;
yes, any custom or protocol."
She wrung her hands as tis she said;
and Per'dur watch them wring instead—
but then bethought him, thanked her politely,
and praised the castle, strong and sightly.

During the meal, a minstrel sang
of an unrequited, love-lost pang,
felt by a knight who didn't speak,
and so his lady was false and weak.
But Peredur with hunger ate
and didn't on singing concentrate;
this tale the minstrel told was lost,
the Breton lai remained unglossed.

And then the king turned to him, said,
"Do you play chess, that boarded spread?
Perhaps, this evening, we can crown
with subtleties of fair renown,
for chess is everywhere acclaimed
for thought that is to action aimed.
And where is greater satisfaction
than 'Checkmate!' crying, in exaction?
Ah yes, to cry out is most good,
most fitting for the eager blood."
Then Peredur replied he played
and would enjoy mock war glissade.

Most faerie was that which followed soon;
for Peredur it had a lacune:
no explanation of the pageant
was made, though he might think it urgent.
What was it came? First, two young men
from one door to another then,
carrying a heavy spear upright
(but slanted, the doors to expedite).
Three streams of blood adown it ran,
dripping off butt diluvian.
Demeanors sober, the bearers two
were plainly dressed in cloth of blue.

The court all glanced at Peredur—
he watched the spear of strange allure.
But no one spoke, nor did he speak:
the spear was borne without critique.
Yet as it left that dining room,
some ladies wept their nation's doom.

Second, two maidens on a salver
carried, sans stumble and sans failure,
from door to door, a human head,
with blood upon the salver red—
a masculine head, with full-grown beard,
with open eyes a-stare, unteared;
a head of some maturity,
but good or evil was hard to see.
The blood was think around its neck:
the blood the silver did bedeck.
Women fearers were dressed in blue,
with plainest cut; unjeweled, too.

Again, the court turned all its glance,
like a primitive hunter throwing his lance,
on Peredur; but he kept silent,
remembering how verbally violent
the king had been when he had spoken,
so concentration on fishing was broken.
But since his rearing had been pious,
Peredur thought, in his own bias,
perhaps Longinus's spear was borne,
and John the Baptist's head so lorn.
(He little felt the gap of time,
the centuries before this mime;
if he'd been told, he would have said
a miracle preserved the head.)

Meanwhile, some women wailed their anguish
that still in drought their state should languish,
and some were helped by maids to leave,
supported, weeping, as they grieved.
The Queen herself, white faced and drawn,
excused herself and soon was gone;
her eyes were red, but never she wept—
one hand its mate quite closely kept.

Therewith, the banquet ended there:
the folk dispersed, the brave, the fair;
the tables were stripped and taken down,
except a small chess-table was found.
The king and Peredur then played
for several hours: in ambuscade
came rooks and knights, the bishops 'tacked,
the queens with power opponents wracked.
At last the king his king had lost;
He sighed and rose, at painful cost,
Congratulated Peredur,
Was helped to leave, to pain perdure.

The young man said the proper things
but thought: "This lord's chess-slaughterings
were not well fought: sometimes most fiercely,
sometimes quite slackly. Perhaps, transpierc'dly
he suffered from his wound, distracted;
I judge him as chess-pieces acted.
He little said, as was most right,
For chess takes concentration quite—
And fore and aft the words were few;
I wonder if me he did eschew?
But, no, it must have been the pain;
The wound is bleeding once again."

So Peredur went soon to bed,
and slept most soundly: on dreams he fed.
But once he woke—one dream disturbed him,
amazed him most and most perturbed him.
He saw the head upon its salver borne,
but in the dream it spoke with scorn;
the tone he knew, but not the words—
the glossolalia seemed absurd;
but still, the tone—the tone was clear:
the inflections carried a verbal sneer.
He woke to find his eyes were wet;
he'd cried his brine in strange regret,
feeling chastised by that dread head,
then sleeping again so visited.

Next morning he rose and took his
horse,

said his farewells and struck a course;
slowly he left that valley dry,
with its gray grasses, unclouded sky.
The lake and castle were far behind him;
he looked not back to straight remind him.
Slowly his gelding climbed to where
leafless trees creaked in springtime air.
Finally, further on, he arrived
where trees had leaves and looked alive;
nearby a thrush was singing, clearly,
its notes like liquid measures purely;
like water dripping, its sang its song—
most like its cousin a continent gone.

This parable sans meaning certain—
its moral masked, hid 'hind a curtain—
(or so it seemed to Peredur)—
was very odd and most obscure.
The game was fairy chess, at least;
strange moves were made with strange caprice.
And Per'dur understood it not:
his wits were dry, with rain no jot.
But if he'd come there less naïve,
who knows what mystery he'd perceive?
Who knows if he'd still seen the head?
or if he had, what it had said?
Reader, think what you will for meaning—
but do not speak what you are weening

SunMoon 2 by **Phillip Fitzsimmons**

The Legend of Halmonga

By Hector Vielva

Part I

When ice began to melt, three black seeds from the first poppy fell. Old Candamu, the Bent-Back, took them and sowed them in the land of his house.

He watched and waited, but they did not sprout.

"What ails you, Old Candamu?" asked Pisuerga, the Mother-River, the Giver of Life.

"They will not grow without your favour, I fear," said Old Candamu woefully.

"Worry not, I shall help you! Yet if a girl is born from one of them, I will keep her, for I need a maiden to care for my banks."

Then the river laid smoothly on the garden. Shortly after, from the first seed emerged a little linden tree. While Old Candamu was opening some furrows, the linden grew and grew until he blocked the light of the sun and the moon. All living and non-living beings complained, so Old Candamu took his axe and set himself to cut down the tree. For three days and nights he hewed and hewed until the linden fell with a loud creak on the Mount Halmonga, creating an enormous crack on the side of the mountain. Fallen branches became the forests that are nowadays at the foot of the Halmonga and surround the villages in the shire.

From the second seed came into being a little ermine. Naughty creature, it did not please Old Candamu, for it was no good for the labour. From the third seed, at last, a young girl was born. Very much pleased with the young girl's vivacious eyes and fine face, Old Candamu wished to take her for his maiden. He named her Cervaria, for that was a land with plenty of deer, and she was beloved by the creatures of the mounts and the creeks, and above all by his friend the ermine. Then came Mother Pisuerga to demand what was hers.

"Behold me! For I am too old of a man, I need someone to care for me and help me to plow," begged the ancient one.

"And yet you agreed, Old Candamu, the Bent-Back," concluded the river.

Old Candamu refused to give away the girl, who was sobbing scared. Rose then Pisuerga and, in its ire, flooded the garden of Old Candamu. The ancient man, uncannily for his age, escaped in a few strides to the slopes of Mount Halmonga. The ermine dragged Cervaria to a nearby mound, though the Mother-River meant them no harm. From that day on, Cervaria became the Maiden of the Water and dwelt in the Cueva Deshondonada. And it is told that she only left the riverbank to visit her dearest ermines, who lived in the ruinous walls where once stood the garden of Old Candamu.

Mount Halmonga, who had seen it all from his heights, did not unlove Old Candamu and allowed him to wander on his slopes. The Bent-Back was for long grumbling and pondering his vengeance against Pisuerga, but his axe would be of no use. Over time, he grew more and more bitter in character, until one day he got lost in the crack that the linden had opened in the side of the Halmonga. Never was he heard of again, and since then he is known as Old Candamu of the Dark Crack.

Part II

Hundreds and hundreds of winters passed until a small town, Cervera, was founded at the foot of Mount Halmonga. Though many different tribes and peoples had come and gone through that shire, it was thus named in honour of Cervaria, the Maiden of the Water, for the folk still remembered the old legend. Then happened something that gave minstrels matter for beautiful songs.

One cold and light morning, the Town Warden's horse appeared at the house door of Al-Mutawir. This young man, one of the barely bearded of Cervera, deemed very strange that the Warden visited his humble house or family. Then he realized that the horse was not tied, for it had come freely. The folk in Cervera knew very well what this meant. According to the old tradition, if the Warden's mount stayed for more than a day and night in front of someone's door, that person should become the new Town Warden. At noon rumours started. When Warden Serabraño found out, firstly he did not believe it, then he disregarded it, and upon dusk he began to worry. Al-Mutawir wished no trouble or foe, so he prayed all night for the bay horse to leave.

Yet at dawn the mount was still there. Al-Mutawir's family convinced him to honour the tradition and claim his right. Not much convinced by these reasons, he was heartened by another motive that he did cherish in his chest. Accompanied by a crowd by now, Al-Mutawir decided to mount the bay horse and made way to the Castle of Cervera. Deep down, Warden Serabraño ardently wished to crush that insolence, but he would not risk unsettling the folk by opposing the custom, for the dastard lords of Vado and Campomunga were always lurking in the boundaries of the shire. He spoke gravely from a turret:

"Welcome Al-Mutawir! For returning my horse have my sincere gratitude."

Al-Mutawir remained stone-silent, full of doubt.

"We all know the tradition, and the tradition has manifested. Well, what have you to say, boy? Speak!"

"My sublime Warden, I do not wish to quarrel with you, but if we are to settle this unexpected sign…"

The young man gathered his courage at last to reveal his most intimate intention:

"…if you allow, I shall request your daughter's hand, the incomparable Brañaflor. Then there will be no further dispute between us, magnanimous chief."

"Obstinate insolent…!" said to himself the Warden in his wrath, but he did not dare to speak in these terms.

Considered Serabraño that it might indeed be a good solution to both hold his authority and not to incite the folk. Besides, he was convinced that he would outwit the young man with an impossible task.

"Alright, Al-Mutawir, but with one condition. To show your courage as the future Town Warden and your worthiness to my dearest daughter, you must climb to the peak of Mount Halmonga."

There were murmurs and whispers of complaint, for even the little children knew that nobody was able to reach the top of the Halmonga in the middle of the winter. Young Brañaflor, who had been listening aside, finally stepped out to see her long-time suitor, for they had desired each other already for several moons.

"I accept!" answered Al-Mutawir.

"At daybreak you shall depart and with the last light we will know, only by a sign of fire, that you have survived," specified Serabraño.

"I shall bring you the very axe of Old Candamu if I must, my chieftain," replied the young man, gazing at the vivid eyes of Brañaflor.

* *
*

Those who are born in the mountains are doomed to restlessly look upon the heights among the fog.

At dawn, Al-Mutawir looks up and believes that the peak of the Halmonga is revealing itself to him. Encouraged by this sign, he is certain that he will have the blessing of the day.

Those who are born in the mountains are obliged to honour the highest.

Mount Halmonga. From below it is believed to be a dwelling of mysteries and primordial secrets. All admire it from afar. It is yet when they consider it a demigod being. But they also dream of raising a hillfort at its foot and be chieftains over the brows and dales.

Those who intend to crown its top break the bound of ancestral homage.

During the climb, Al-Mutawir realizes that the peak is not invincible nor divine and, when reaching the top, his sight finally rules over the High Basin of Pisuerga and the whole valley. However, after that moment of euphoria, he suspects that the old mountain is barely tolerating his presence. Suddenly he finds himself surrounded by rocks and crags with human shapes.

"Are these the ones that tried it before me?", says he to himself, bewildered.

A voice emerges from the bosom of the earth like a slow cataclysm:

"I, WHO HAVE SEEN THE COMINGS AND GOINGS OF THE LIVING AND THE NON-LIVING, ERE MEN AND AFTER MEN AND WILL DO SO… HARK, AL-MUTAWIR, I AWAIT YOUR FALL FOR YOU ARROGANCE!"

Terrified by the mountain blare that is cracking the rocks around him, the young man regrets his previous thoughts and regains his initial modesty. Deep inside him a new form of homage to the great mount is born. It is neither a being to be worshipped nor a fortress to dominate the others, but the imperishable guardian of the valley. In the heart of Al-Mutawir, the bound with the mountain becomes one of a profound respect, an admiration without superstition, and a sincere love for every crag, stone, and tree. And it is only then when Mount Halmonga begins to love him. The last light of the day falls inexorably and below the folk wait, staring at the peak. Brañaflor shivers like a folded poppy flower. Finally falls the dark and everyone holds their breaths. Before the Town Warden claims his victory, a flame trembles on the top of the mountain.

* *
*

Following his derring-do, Al-Mutawir, The One who Climbed, eventually united with Brañaflor and one day he became the Town Warden of Cervera. But until then, he continued plowing the land under the caring look of Mount Halmonga.

Two Souls on a Shore
By Geoffrey Reiter

The elf and the Kuparean man were hungry as they walked along the shore of the island. They did not remain at the rock-choked shallows that had disemboweled their trireme. The merchant crew of the eagle-prowed Protaro lay mangled amid the mingled kelp and flotsam. The survivors did not look back at those swollen, cold bodies, though they did not march with as much expedience as they might have.

When they had ambled unsteadily some three hundred spans along the uneven shore, the elf turned to the Kuparean and, for the first time since the wreck, she spoke. "We must find sustenance," she told him.

The Kuparean turned to face her, his eyes the deep brown of late dusk. "It is late in the season. We'll not find fish this far from the deeps." He pursed his lips, as if dreading the implications of his words.

"Then we must seek food inland," the elf responded.

The Kuparean did not speak. He gazed at the Toparian Ocean, watched longingly its passionate inhalations and exhalations beneath the sunset-blushed clouds. He shuffled a leather-clad foot in the crumbling grey sand. The he turned toward the rocky, moss-crusted cliff, and, after a moment's hesitation, he started up the steep acclivity. The elf began side-by-side with him, but with her steady step upon the limestone, she soon outpaced him. Her lithe limbs, trained on the glaciers of Zehrish, navigated the calcified nooks of chalky elevation. Soon, the Kuparean watched her long, snowy hair and sealskin buskin disappear over the arc of the precipice.

"Hold, Hrinē!" he shouted, and his deep voice rebounded over the rock.

Her pale green face peered back over the ledge.

"I know your feet favor the undulations of the ocean, Yaru," she replied in a voice of calculated patience. "But we must discover sustenance before the sun blazes down the horizon."

Yaru renewed his effort, awkwardly grappling with the intransigent rock. As he neared the overhang at the top of the cliff, Hrinē's slender, powerful hand closed around his own. She pulled him over the ledge until he stood beside her on the summit.

Yaru looked around. Before them stood a small, dense grove, around which grew quince and pomegranate. They formed a tight ring in the midst of the earth that covered the cliff summit.

"There will be food here," Hrinē said quietly, stoically.

"Yes," nodded Yaru. He stroked the thin bristles of his beard with a thick hand, the color of the obsidian sands on Kuparea's southeastern shore. The sinking red sun's rays cooled, chilling the sweat on the back of his neck. He and Hrinē started toward the grove.

The trees were thick, yet there were evident signs of pruning, of sophisticated horticulture. Fruit had recently been removed from the branches. The two sailors paused silently, but necessity urged them onward. Despite the density of growth, there were avenues of passage through the thicket, and pushing aside aggressive branches, they moved deeper into the grove.

After a few strides, the undergrowth thinned out abruptly, and Yaru and Hrinē found themselves in a clearing at the heart of the grove. It was a circular space ringed with a mound of earth that held back the trees and shrubs. In the very center, they saw a pole of cypress rising to the height of the trees, as though aimed to pierce the roseate clouds in the deepening sky above. They could see minute detail carved into the pole, writhing figures—some human, some beast—

contorting in impossible, suggestive poses, linked to one another by ties natural and unnatural. And beside the pole, there stood a man.

His features were ancient and broken. The ruddy flesh of his countenance was desiccated, cracked and flaking, though too dry to peel. He had an animalistic, simian likeness: dry, bulbous, baboon-like nose, cloud-shrouded night eyes, and wide, powerful jaws. His hunched figure was draped in a robe that had once clearly glittered like souls in the evening but had since faded and tattered over his shoulders. In his withered, mottled hands, he held a staff that may have been a shepherd's crook, though its head had cracked off, leaving only sharp wooden splinters on top.

"What brings you to my sanctuary?" he asked with a voice like a grist mill. His language was a bastardized form of old Briscuin, syllables leaning on each other like the house-frames of a shanty town. Yaru and Hrinē, with their traders' understanding of foreign tongues, could just make out what he said.

"We intended no trespass," replied Yaru in the most ancient Briscuin he knew, his voice soft like distant thunder over the waves. "Our craft grounded on this island's shore. We want only food and drink."

The old man's eyes squinted, and he moved slowly toward the two interlopers. They could hear a crackling, the sound of old bone breaking beneath his sandaled feet.

"What is mine is mine!" he shouted in a voice of brittle sandstone. "How can you have it, what is mine?"

And he raised his splintered staff in a hand cracked like dried sugar cane. In the sight of Yaru and Hrinē, the grove seemed to wrinkle and fold like papyrus. The old man's voice crumbled through the clearing, and he pronounced, "Interlopers you, let you be imprisoned in your selves. Away!"

In Yaru's starlit ocean eyes, the old man and the pole and the clearing in the heart of the trees seemed to wash away, like the erosion of a cliffside. His view was replaced by a thick darkness. But the darkness was not empty. It was turbulent, tempestuous, chaotic. For a moment, he was comforted. He imagined the cedar of the Protaro beneath his leather boots, the familiar swell of near limitless water spread out beneath the boat. He imagined the mounting winds from gathering clouds, a storm approaching like a gift. He imagined the grace of lightning, the paternal whisper of thunder, the shattering life of an autumnal squall.

But there was no deck to separate his feet from the churning waves of night. It devoured him, swallowed him, engulfed him. He groped about in the ravening abyss, but his scarred fingers found no purchase. Yet somehow, the jaws of the impenetrable gulf tore at him, shook him through to the marrow of each bone. The darkness stole the breath from his lungs. He felt his whole person being battered about by the riptide of chaos.

And somewhere across the depths, Hrinē watched as the ancient heathen seemed to attenuate into pure geometry. Organic curves and contours resolved into blindingly precise shapes before and around her. Their crystalline purity shone like the dawn over the ice sheet of Sezir Bay. There was comfort in the cold, hard figures crossing before her eyes, like the arms of her father crossed in front of her.

But then the pale, perpendicular lines continued to constrict. The embrace of angles, the hug of precision, tightened around her like an ill-fitting sarcophagus. The glistering parallelograms crushed the air from her lungs, stung her vertebrae, noosed her neck. The dragnet of squares enmeshed her flesh, dug deeply into her soft green skin. She opened her mouth to scream, and the polyhedrons poured down her throat like vertical shafts of rain.

In disorderly panic, Hrinē struggled against the bondage of her nature. With a wild impulse beyond all arithmetic, she loosed her left hand, flailing it out into the void beyond her prison.

50

And beyond the suffocating balance of her diagrammed soul, she felt in her empty palms a new pressure. It was quite unlike the stifling force of her convictions. This pressure was malleable, sweaty, organic. This pressure was strong and wild with life. It was the hand of Yaru.

For Yaru, in the nauseous gulf whirling about him, had thrust his right arm sharply through the billowing mass, cutting the chaos with an acute discipline. And far past his vision, he felt the cold, slender, desperate hand of Hrinē the elf.

When the hands of Yaru and Hrinē embraced across the distance of two spans and a vast animate expanse of selves, their prisons melted and began to drain away. Yaru felt a gentle force shaping and containing the depths his soul had generated. Hrinē beheld the defined angles before her as they were made vital and asymmetrical by true and turbulent life. And they beheld again the little grove and the brittle, baffled mage.

His squinting, feral eyes fell wide open as the two mariners, hand in hand, slowly walked toward him. He uttered a hoarse, rattling scream of disbelief. Taking his broken rod in hand, he started to advance upon Yaru and Hrinē. But even as he took his first step, the old man's eroded flesh began to flake and crumble away. Like a coastal bluff battened by the relentless crests of ocean and the vertical force of rain, his chalky escarpment of a face cracked and tumbled down a piece at a time. He made it six paces before his frame fractured and collapsed completely, leaving a pile of ashy fragments, draped in a soiled robe.

Still holding hands, Yaru and Hrinē walked forward into the grove. They did not stop to look at the desiccated remnants of the shrouded sorcerer, and the odor of his ruin did not even ascend to their sense. Without even exchanging words, the two reached the pole in the center of the grove. Together, they kicked at the old carven monument. Its rotten base caved and gave way, and it toppled down to the earth. Then, as the last vestiges of twilight faded away and the great soul-sea of crystalline night emerged, the Kuparean and the elf made their way to the nearest tree and at last ate the fruit from its branches.

Bird in the Branches by Leigh Ann Brook

A Poem by Jonathan Rolfe

The Three Kindreds

High are the Elves, and high their works,
And bright was Earth beneath their hand,
And beauty filled the Western World
When Elven virtue wreathed the land.
Their dwellings in the tow'ring trees,
From mountains' knees to western shore;
Their minds beyond a mortal's ken,
The world by them was blest, of yore.

Deep are the Dwarves,   and deep their works,
Their dwellings carven   in deep caverns;
In their fiery forges   and profound smithies
Blows of hammers   were like bells ringing,
Deep underground,   in days of yore.
Long were their beards,   long their memories:
Mighty in vengeance,   mindful of friendship.
Dear was their treasure,   in the deeps of time.

But far and wide across the earth
The Men have spread, and so their works.
The Middle Children pass away,
and mortal Men must now hold sway.
All Elven beauty fades and falls;
No hammer rings in Dwarven halls.
"The forge's fire is ashen-cold;"*
The world is fallen from the glory of old.

But memory lives on, in song and tale:
The flame of former days shall never fail.

*LOTR II, 4

Alrond and the Magic Fox

By Evgeny A. Khvalkov

Have you heard the story of Alrond and the magic fox? I can tell it to you.

After all, magic foxes still live in some corners of the world to this day. It is almost impossible to catch them because they are very strong in magic. And sometimes, when such a fox runs through the forest and touches the branches and bushes with his tail, sparks fly from the tail to the sky and fall back to the ground; people call these sparks shooting stars. However, sometimes magic foxes appear among people. This is what our story will be about.

Once upon a time, there was an old knight who lived at Cape Bertoari, and he had three sons. When the old man died, the eldest son inherited the castle and all the land, according to the custom, the middle son inherited the parish in the village and the post of a priest, and the youngest, Alrond, only got his father's sword and an old horse. The elder brother gave Alrond a loaf of bread and a ham for the journey and told him to go away to seek his fortune somewhere else.

Alrond got ready and thought about going to Adtiarn to the court of King Taravon. He, people say, pays the brave and clever nobles handsomely. And Alrond went to the city of Adtiarn.

Some time passed, and Alrond grew tired and hungry and sat down to eat at the edge of the forest. Lo and behold, a fox's face poked out from behind a viburnum bush. The fox looks at Alrond, and Alrond looks at the fox. And the fox said to him:

"Good afternoon, young man! Nice ham you've got there. Would you share a piece?"

And though Alrond had no other food left but that bread and ham, he was a good fellow, so he gave the fox a piece of ham and told him how his brothers had treated him and that he was going to Adtiarn to the court of King Taravon.

"Look," said the fox, "maybe I should go with you to try my luck too? You are a good fellow, I see, but you are very simple-minded, and I am well versed in all sorts of tricks, and perhaps I can also serve you. And when we get to Adtiarn, you'll join King Taravon's guard, and I'll be an interpreter for Chancellor Berengar. I know all sorts of languages: Garegin, Adelnian, and even the language of the Igerulds."

"Well," said Alrond, "it's more fun to walk the road together. Come with me!"

And they went to the city of Adtiarn. Then they came, and King Taravon hired our Alrond as his personal guard, for the captain of the guards was an old friend of the young man's late father, and Alrond took after his father in face, courage, and intelligence. And the fox settled down at the chancery and surprised everyone with his knowledge of languages: the scribes, the councilors, the chancellor, and the king himself were surprised and amazed by the fox's wisdom.

The king had a marriageable daughter. As soon as she saw Alrond, she fell madly in love with him; the young man was also not indifferent to the princess. But it was a custom in the kingdom that not only could the princess not choose the man dear to her heart at her discretion, but even the father-king himself could not, as is the case in most all kingdoms, arrange his daughter's marriage according to his whim. There had to be a great contest, and whoever came out victorious must also receive the princess's hand. And since the princess was a marriageable lady, and the only daughter of King Taravon, and the king himself was already in his old age, the chancellor and the councilors began to bother him so that he would soon arrange a contest and wed the princess to the winner.

"We want," they said, "to have a suitable successor to you—a glorious, valiant, intelligent, and in every way worthy prince or knight; we do not need any other kind of king!"

The king had to give in and arrange a contest. Alrond came back home from the service sad, and the fox asks him:

"Why are you so sad, my friend? Why do you look so crestfallen?"

"How can I not be sad!" answered Alrond "The king has declared a contest, and whoever wins it will receive the princess's hand, and my beloved will become a foreigner's wife."

"Why don't you take part in the competition?" said the fox. "Although your father was a poor knight, and you are even poorer, your family is noble and your ancestry is not inferior to the king's. Moreover, you are a man of strength and ingenuity!"

"True," said Alrond, "but I feel that the trials there will not be the usual ones: not fighting with a spear, shooting a bow or wielding a sword."

"But you have me! I'll help you through the royal trials," said the fox.

Alrond gave it some thought and agreed. And the fox waved his tail, and golden sparks fell on the young man—and although Alrond had been handsome before and such a daredevil as there were few, now he shone with a magical light, and he had the strength of thirty strong men.

When the time came for the contest, kings, princes, dukes, counts, barons, and knights from all over the West Coast, and some even from the islands of the Archipelago, came to Adtiarn. The first three days were spent in tournaments, hunting, and feasting, and Alrond was ahead of the others in all things: in spear-fighting, sword-fighting, archery, crossbow shooting, and dancing, and he was behaving so courteously—as a true suitor for a princess! But the royal trials were more difficult than the court dances.

It was time for the first contest. And the king said:

"Last year, the Duke Larhelm of Moremont gave me some wonderful seeds that produce a harvest of five hundred, and bread made from that wheat has such wonderful properties that one small piece is enough to feed an adult man. My peasants sowed this miraculous grain in the fields, and indeed, the harvest was unprecedented. But what a misfortune: someone comes at night and eats the wheat. And when I send the guards to catch the unknown thief, they all fall asleep. Which of you, glorious knights, will protect my fields of wonder wheat and at the same time, catch the mysterious robber and bring him to me?"

All the kings, princes, dukes, earls, barons, and knights were perplexed, and so was Alrond. He came home and told the fox about the royal mission. And the fox said:

"I know who steals the wheat—it's the proboscis monster. Follow my advice, get a good night's sleep, and let's go watch the thief at night. Just don't forget to plug your ears."

So they did. And when at night all the kings, princes, dukes, counts, barons, and knights went out to guard the field, the proboscis monster came up to it and trumpeted his trunk—then everybody fell asleep. Alrond covered his ears, as the fox had told him, and did not fall asleep. As soon as the thief began to graze on the royal fields, Alrond and the fox began to catch the proboscis monster. For a long while, they could not cope with it until the fox jumped on the monster and threw a rope on it.

In the morning, Alrond brought the proboscis monster to the king. The king was surprised, and praised and thanked Alrond. The foreign kings, princes, dukes, counts, barons and knights became envious: they slept all night while Alrond and the fox caught the monster! And they plotted against Alrond, but they did not show it.

It was time for the second contest. And the king said:

"Last year King Aethelstan of Damyria gave me a flock of golden-fleeced sheep. Now it's time to shear them. Their wool is pure gold, but I must say that these sheep are very skittish, and so far no one has managed to shear them. Which of you, glorious knights, can shear the sheep and gather the golden wool and bring it to me?"

All the kings, princes, dukes, earls, barons, and knights were perplexed, and so was Alrond. He came home and told the fox about the royal mission. And the fox said:

"That is not difficult, my friend Alrond. Follow my advice, get a good night's sleep, and tomorrow we'll go and shear the golden-fleeced sheep."

In the morning, the pretenders to the princess's hand began to catch the golden-fleeced sheep, but they were very quick and skittish, and no one managed to cut a piece of golden wool from them. It was Alrond's turn at last. Then the fox, his faithful friend, sat down on the hillock where the sheep were grazing, took out his flute, and began to play. Oh, if you could only imagine what kind of music it was! All the sheep gathered around the fox and listened to the magic music as if they were enchanted, and now it was easy for Alrond to shear them.

And not only the sheep were enchanted! The clear sound of that music enchanted the king, the courtiers, the retinue, and everybody who were there; they all fell silent and listened as if in a daze. Wild forest animals came out of their holes and dens to listen to the wonderful music of the fox. The lion, the king of all beasts, dared not growl lest he should interrupt the wondrous music, the wolf forgot his howl, and the auroch forgot his roar. Even old Greta, who lives at the Break-in-the-Moat and is famous for the worst character (she can't do without scolding others even for one minute), so even old Greta herself came out and listened to the music. The melody that the fox produced from his flute turned everything into a temple of music.

The King was thrilled that Alrond had completed the second task and doubly thrilled that he had heard such magical music. He sincerely thanked Alrond and the fox, and the foreign kings, princes, dukes, counts, barons, and knights almost burst with envy and anger. And one of them, King Gerneb of Lothirod, said:

"If this knight passes the third contest, he will have the princess, and we will leave unrewarded and even disgraced, and some poor soldier will be higher than us, crowned heads! We'll ambush him tomorrow morning before the third trial and kill him, and thus we won't have to suffer dishonor."

They all decided to do so. But they did not know that the fox was standing behind the curtain and heard everything. He came home and told Alrond about the insidious plans of the foreigners.

"What should I do then?" said the young man.

"Trust me", the fox replied, "but just remember that tomorrow we have to both defeat our enemies and to pass the last contest!"

It was time for the third and final contest. And the king said:

"I want my future son-in-law to treat me to a sumptuous dinner in his own castle, and this reception has to be royal! I will not marry my daughter to a beggar."

Foreign kings, princes, dukes, counts, barons, and knights were alarmed. Of course, they had magnificent palaces and castles in their region—but you can't take a king there in one day, nor can you bring these palaces and castles to Adtiarn, no matter how hard you work! However, the four richest kings hired a hundred masons each and ordered them to build castles near the capital at once—but you can't build a castle in a day! Alrond looked sad, but the fox nudged him and said:

"I'll go and get you a castle for the king's party, and when you go hunting now, keep away from the foreigners!"

And the fox ran in the direction of Cromorgan Castle. And I must say that this castle was owned by a terrible troll, most despicable, evil and cruel. Many travellers who passed by Cromorgan Castle ended up in the teeth of that ugly ogre. But the troll ate humans and not foxes, so our dodger had nothing to fear; besides, the troll was not at home at that time—he had gone out to hunt. First of all, the fox decided to get rid of the troll's servants who guarded the castle; those were gnoll Graw, goblin Grow and gremlin Grahaham. He ran to the gate and shouted:

"Alarm! Run for your lives! Here comes the king with his army and brings with him a hundred wizards: they will burn you all to ashes with their lightnings!"

The troll's servants were alarmed. What should they do? And the fox told them:

"Hide quickly; maybe the king and his army and wizards will not notice you!"

The troll's servants were cowardly, so they left their guard posts without a moment's delay. The gnoll Graw hid in a beer keg, the goblin Grow hid in a wine barrel, and the gremlin Grahaham hid in a cask of calvados (the troll was very fond of calvados). Then our fox closed them all up, rolled them out on the fortress wall and threw them into the moat—let them swim there!

Meanwhile, the evil troll, the master of the house, returned and was quite surprised that his servants are gone and that a strange fox had appeared out of nowhere in his own castle. But our fox was an extremely courteous gentleman, so he had no difficulty in charming the troll. Knowing that the troll is very fond of flattery, the fox began to describe in every possible way the merits of the troll and his glorious fame in all the surrounding kingdoms.

I must add that this troll had two heads, and they often quarreled with each other. And here's what the fox came up with—he repeatedly paid more and more colorful compliments to one head or the other, until finally they got into a big quarrel and locked in a deadly battle. Then the fox crept softly to where the troll kept his sharp, curved sabers, like those which camelmen use in the desert for a fight, and with a deft blow cut off both of the evil troll's quarrelsome heads. And since then, no one has ever captured or killed travelers in those parts!

Meanwhile, King Taravon hunted with his courtiers, retinue, and foreign kings, princes, dukes, earls, barons, and knights, who, as you will remember, plotted to kill Alrond. In pursuit of a deer, Alrond broke away from the entire retinue and was left alone, and then the foreigners began chasing him. Their swords were drawn, their crossbows loaded, and that would have been the end of the young man if he hadn't had his fox!

And the fox, after taking possession of the magnificent castle of the villainous troll and giving orders to prepare a real royal feast, hurried to the forest where the hunt was going on. At that time, there was a very old, dilapidated bridge in this forest. So, when the enemies were chasing Alrond and shooting at him with crossbows, the fox (and he was a magic fox, after all!) briefly transformed his friend into a fox and hid him in a burrow, while the fox himself turned into a young man, just like Alrond—you wouldn't even tell one from another! The foreign kings, princes, dukes, earls, barons, and knights rushed after him, and the fox in the guise of Alrond leapt from his horse and ran across the old bridge to the other side. The foreigners, thinking that their victim was in their hands, rushed after him to the dilapidated bridge, and the bridge collapsed, so they all perished.

Meanwhile, the king was hungry and was waiting for dinner. The fox restored Alrond to his human form and himself to his fox form, and they returned to the king.

"Your Majesty," the fox said, "Sir Alrond has the honor to invite you to dine at his castle.

The king was surprised. "How come, Alrond? Your father's castle is ten days' ride from here, and it belongs to your elder brother by right of the entail."

"I assure you, Sire," the fox said, "that Sir Alrond has a castle, and a most magnificent one."

And the fox led Alrond, the king, and the entire king's retinue to the castle of Cromorgan, which had once belonged to the evil troll, and now it belonged to the fox's friend, knight Alrond. When they reached the castle, the king was overjoyed, for Cromorgan Castle was as good as a royal palace, and the reception that the fox and Alrond provided for the king and his retinue there was truly royal. The king was quite charmed, and at the same dinner he announced the betrothal of Alrond and the Princess, and appointed Alrond as heir to the throne.

What about the magic fox? Well, the fox, when the wedding was over, took his leave and ran into the forest; after all, he was a wild animal, although later he sometimes came to visit his friend.

That's it, my friends! Alrond did not spare the last thing he had for the fox, and in the end he became king.

Two In One

primordial androgyny and the singing head of Orpheus

by David Sparenberg

As I looked to the high ground, which was indeed shaped in the semblance of a sublime albeit miniature mountain, imagine my amazement to hold in view the monumental figure of a curious two-headed deity. Or if not a form divine—replete with numinous aura—then at least a presence late emerged from the narrative realms of mythology, or from out the twilight sphere of dream visiting archetypes. Immediately my thought turned to the double-faced god, Janus of Rome.

Only the personage I beheld was of a more intimate nature than a roll of dice or crystal ball, deciphering of sheep's entrails or the reading of Tarot spread on a gypsy's nomadic table. A towering nude: the head to one side was distinctively male, bearded with chiseled features, while the other was clearly female, delicate and with soft complexion. So too the colossal body

Sunflowers for OLA **by Phillip Fitzsimmons**

One side of the torso was masculine and muscled for hunting and the hefting of stone, with the complimentary half of feminine breasted curves expressing intuitive persuasion, nurturing, and captivating sensuality. Likewise, the legs, long and shapely according to their gender, while at the groin were planted organs of each sex, as if shaded flowers of contrary but complementary variety; symbols of an anatomical anomaly, only to be wondered at on a nonconsensual level of a prodigious anatomy! The image represented to my imagination was an illusion of self-fertilization, an erogenous monad. Or else a Platonic symbolization of primordial non-duality. Surreal was the attraction of this monstrous beauty!

From around that form of living symmetry shone out a feathered glow of gold and silver light in undulant equipoise. Such was as if both sun and moon, as single force combined, radiated from behind the awe instilling vision. A sight most rare, utterly sublime, and simultaneously awesome! The transhuman is often shocking to normal human sensibilities. We have grown numb and now unheeding of the numen is manifested!

As I beheld, out of a cause mysteriously concealed beyond the reach of ordinary reason, my thoughts flew away to the wild Thracian poet Orpheus, whose acts of beauty, as tales are told, this is to say, whose shamanic empowered poetry displayed a charm to transform objects hard and intended for harm into merry butterflies, soft frogs, and multicolored, miniature dragons, winged reptiles with eyes like limpid pools and breath of meadow flowers. Whose power of poetic art, I strive to tell you, was of such enchantment as to subvert even the adamantine heart of Hades, Lord of the Underworld, and don to all roaming shadows of malignancy, panic, and night terrors. Orpheus—gifted (blessed and cursed), Orpheus—who perished under the forest-scented hands of his godfather Dionysus' maenads, repeating the initiation of shamanic dismemberment, and whose severed head continued to sing of natural raptures as it floated off upon serpentine, subconscious waters.

Somehow, from down in depths of a collectively shared imagination, I must have stood remembering a kindred bond between the troubadour of metamorphic prowess and my mound-vision of the two souled and double sexed deity—the whispered hermaphrodite or psyche's androgyny. Under compression of an outwardly strange and inwardly exhilarating emotional alchemy, there feels to me to be a sacred merging of these two entities into one—one singular and profound identity. Is it not at such a radical (erotic) union of consciousness and unconscious content that identity becomes destiny?

Perhaps, when I might dream Big again, it would best please my soul that I should dream into conscious patterns the offspring of this provocative union—a wing-enraptured human sphere, a mandala-spirit of creative potency, with blissful countenance, as should be found now only on such as dancing Shiva, with lap-seated Shakti integrated into a smooth interior harmony—shaped complete, in eternal union, and empowered equally with blood and thunder and the mystic hues of gender-accepting elegance, a poetic of dreaming and lingering in cosmic serenity.

Pick up a pebble, please, and see how it rounds itself and reminds us through smallness of Earth's uplifting mountains. Pick up a seed and observe how seed does the same and suggests to our second naivety the rightness of things and sensations, showing how in this small compact of energy is held for the appropriate season the promised treasure of a numinous forest or Earth-mystical orchard. Druids through the ages have come to study in those vaults of initiation.

Wonder with me, lingering in our Earth-walk narrative: Of what did the sailing head of Orpheus sing, if not of depths of peace and passion, of breathing spheres, as round as ever was temptation's smiling apple, botanical, nautical, ecstatic-erotic, of miracles, of death, of returning, the veil and cloud, of nightingales of naked beauty and attested moments fertile with eternal gold and glory?

Never, never, never once did the Orphic voice, like phoenix out of ashes, assent to murder, attend the sinister betrayals of torture; never in the vital dynamic of balance consent to cutting down, breaking off and executing the desire of life through disrespectful greed and aggressive violence. Those are but tools and weapons of dread and antagonistic fragments of obstruction, cast forth to disrupt universal continuance. These, the Orphic, emergent spheres out of multiverses, are more delightful and proceed to centering. This does not stop with flesh of any single body, but rather flows outward in waves of energies to land and waters, atmosphere and sky. Is this process not to give form, shaded with timeless features, to deeper, more ancient strata of organic intricacies and intimate bonding—where but in the grounding dimension of Being's openness? A constellation unearthed by depth psychology; an evolutionary puzzle piece to be fitted into contemporary relevance and our nascent ecosophy? We discover the evolution of identity through vision and recovery: a wild double facing god, giver-and-taker of light and dark, the androgynous psyche of species maturity and the subversive, singing shepherd Orpheus—inspirational touchstones for the enlightening achievement of an Ecozoic future!

Flowers in Glass for Tolkien by Phillip Fitzsimmons

Taliessen in the Rose Garden by Joseph Thompson

A Poem by Krista Canterbury Adams

Wood Witches

This fir wood
Burns down to a dark incense.

We watch from the window—sunset
On the pale water-lights
Of the river
Where the river banks burn bright
With moss and flowers.
This gold drips,
This last of light.

In the window
Your scarves, patterned in silver,
Green and crimson red,
Drift like gauze in the evening wind,
Sifting this archaic city
Into patterned, opaque, translucent, clear.

This morning in the market
We bought an hourglass
Of painted bone—
It sits now on the sill,
Slipping sand,
Losing time—against
Soft, warm evening sky.

With the breath of the great, overhanging cypress
We let its sand run out,
Turn it over many times,
And night stretches on.

This morning in the market
We passed over many mirrors—filigreed,
embossed,
Silver and gold—
Examined thick spheres
Of jet, of amber. Touched the perfect crystal
Perched on silver—
Twisted, textured,
Like ancient pewter roots,
Or like branches.

We grimaced,
Imagined the old wood witch,
Deep in the dark fir forest,
Hammering out her rare
And various metals,
Toes curled like snails in the mud.

How the Dryad and the Naiad Got or Didn't Get Together

By Kevan Kenneth Bowkett

1.

Once, in the river-land of Sopenya, near Lake Chellu, there lived a naiad and a dryad. They were a boy and a girl, respectively.

One day the naiad boy's mother was saying: "Our son is the only boy of First Clan Tharquem, and that dryad girl is the only girl of Branch Silasi. They should get married!"

"But there are naiad girls in our Clan Tharquem," said her husband reasonably, looking up from his newspaper which, since they were underwater, was written with indelible inks on oiled guanaco-skin. "And there are dryad boys in her Branch Silasi."

"Don't complicate matters, husband!" cried the naiad-wife. "The *Book of Marriages of Wood and River* says there should be at least one cross-marriage every half-century."

"Complicate matters? Not me," said her husband. "I just mention complications already present."

"See, there!" she said. "You're making it more complicated already!"

He thought of making a further comment, then shrugged and turned over the guanaco-skin. He thought upon the next book he'd ordered that was due soon to arrive—it was an expensive book, its words and images etched on beautiful bones.

The naiad mother called her son in and asked him, "Don't you think Soloonwa Dryad's-daughter is lovely?"

"Yes, very lovely, mother," he replied.

"Wouldn't you like to marry her?" she asked.

"No, mother," he said. "I'm not in love with her."

It ended in an argument.

Meanwhile, in Dryad's Bower, the dryad father was speaking to his wife. "Our girl is at marriageable age, dear," he said.

"And will be for a long time to come," she rustled in reply (for she was in tree form). "There's no rush."

"But there's a best moment for the bee to tread the blossom," said the dryad father. "And it isn't deep into spring either."

Dryad mother rustled again. "There's still no rush. She'll have a good long spring."

"But what about the *Book of Marriages of River and Wood*?" he quaked (for he was an aspen, and had just reverted to his tree shape). "Isn't one of those weddings due?"

"What's that to do with our daughter?" she murmured, assuming human shape and sitting down on a mossy stone.

"Well, I was thinking, the sapling might like to marry the naiad son of First Clan Tharquem," he trembled, his leaves rippling.

"Well, ask her and find out!" said the mother.

Then they called their daughter Soloonwa and when she came her father asked whether she thought Merzan, the naiad son of Clan Tharquem, was handsome.

"Oh, pa," she said, "he's not handsome, he's gorgeous."

"Ah, then," continued her father, glancing at his wife with a look that said, *See how well we progress*, "then—would you not like to marry him?"

"Marry him! Oh, no, pa! I'm not in love with him."

"What's that got to do," he began—then stopped, for his marriage with the dryad mother had been a love match.

He reasoned, however, that many matches among the dryads and the naiads were arranged ones. Why, some of the dryad marriages were even arranged by the bees! So at his insistence, he and his wife sent a message to the naiads, to the mother and father of young Merzan of First Clan Tharquem, requesting that they be permitted to call. Naiad-father saw little point in it, but added, "Well, we needn't have a point to visit with our friends, need we, my dear? Naiads and dryads have been calling on each other since the days humans were banished from this country. If not before, I rather think, if not before. Let them come." And naiad-mother smiled, and kept her purposes to herself, and sent back a welcome.

The two couples had tea together, in human form, although from time to time one of them would revert to tree or water shape for a change, and to restore their strength.

Naiad-mother and dryad-father quickly found a shared interest in the *Book of Marriages* and, while their spouses rolled their eyes and smiled, the two of them made a plan of campaign to get their respective children wed to each other, starting with picnics and parties, and proceeding, if required, to journeying together and then, if absolutely necessary, to cajolings, weepings, threats, and kidnappings.

"That's extreme," rustled dryad-mother, standing decoratively by a stream bank (she was a rowan). "I put my root down at kidnapping."

"And I my flipper!" cried naiad-father, in the shape of a pool in a grassy hollow delicately reflecting the sky.

The matchmakers proceeded with their modified plan of campaign. They got other members of their respective clans lined up behind their intentions, and began a season of at-homes, fetes, walking, swimming, standing in the wind, and even picnics on the Sopenya pampas beyond the edge of the woods. Naiad-mother and dryad-father and their allies were at times encouraged by the extent to which their son and daughter could be seen together, frequently flushed and laughing; they deemed it would only take time for their aim to be fulfilled. They would perhaps have been less sanguine had they known that what provoked such laughter was most often the ridiculous antics of the matchmakers in throwing the couple together.

One evening, from behind a periodical with sheets made of kelp from the Golden Inlet, the naiad husband said, "Do you think your matrimonial plans will work, my dear? After all, our son Merzan is such an excellent naiad, and young Soloonwa is such an excellent dryad—and marrying out of species is hardly commonplace for such excellences."

"That shows how much you know," replied the naiad wife. "The *Book of Marriages of Wood and River* is full of stories in which typically excellent naiads wed typically excellent dryads. It's part of their excellence to do so."

The naiad husband, defeated, puffed noisily on his steam-pipe and turned to the page of sales and auctions, beginning to consider buying a freshwater-seahorse pen that he didn't need, to soothe his wounded feelings.

The season of parties and picnics went by without producing any noticeable inclination of Soloonwa the young dryad to wed Merzan, the young naiad.

So sterner stuff was tried: the two were chosen and sent as messengers to a gathering of their respective peoples in the northern mountains. It was an arduous journey, and the couple were together in difficult circumstances for several months.

But on returning, and being asked whether they were now inclined toward each other, Merzan and Soloonwa burst out laughing, and said no more.

So their respected parents moved on to the cajolery; this failing, they went on to the weepings, the grindings of teeth, the divination purporting to show this marriage was the will of the gods, then threats of expulsion or of being excluded from their parents' wills.

"Go ahead," Merzan said to his mother, chuckling. "It's not like the streams will run out of fish."

"It won't bother me," said Soloonwa, shaking her ash-coloured locks.

"We won't let you share our sun," said her father sternly.

"She shines everywhere, I'll manage," answered Soloonwa.

One day a water rat came to Dryad's Bower to announce that Merzan was gone, vanished, and please could the dryads help look for him?

They helped—but to no avail. Merzan had disappeared from the forest.

So First Clan Tharquem of the naiads summoned a magician of their people, a mighty sorcerer who dwelt in Chelmirau Pool. He came, and performed a potent incantation, imploring the spirits of the five elements to seek for Merzan. And at the end of it he said impressively, "Merzan has been carried to an oasis in the Western Desert by a foul sand lich. He cannot flee, lest he dry up ere he reaches other water." There were murmurs and cries and wringing of fins and fronds among those present. The magician jabbed his finger toward Soloonwa and cried,

"You, Soloonwa! You are the one the Powers deem most suited to send to him and bring him home."

"Now why doesn't that surprise me?" she murmured softly as a breeze sighed through her branches.

She set our westward, had many adventures, hit upon a method of crossing the desert sands without drying up and dying, by making herself a thick coat and shoes of mosses, hornworts, and liverworts, and found the oasis in question. It was an extensive one, surrounded by a ruined city. Merzan was living in a pool in the midst of a pavement of broken, faded lapis-lazuli stones.

Soloonwa and Merzan put their heads together, thought of how to frighten off the sand lich, and did so. The lich was much easier to scare away than either had supposed. All they need do was hide behind a broken pediment and, when it came by, leap out and cry "Shoo!" and it vanished away into the desert.

They laughed, and set off across the sands, travelling at night. Soloonwa kept Merzan hydrated and alive by allowing him to drink some of her sap from time to time. They had many adventures along the way, but they returned safe to the watered lands and to the woods of their home.

When Merzan and Soloonwa had settled back in to their usual pursuits, the naiad's mother perceived that her son was grateful to Soloonwa Dryad's-daughter for rescuing him, but no nearer to proposing to her.

"It's really a dripping shame," said naiad-mother after Merzan had declined for the dozenth time to go and propose to Soloonwa. "After I practically bled water to arrange that he be abducted so the girl would have to go and rescue him!"

Naiad-father heard that, and there were scenes.

"How could you arrange to kidnap our son!" he shouted. "I see it all now—don't I know that sand lich is an old ally of your mother's family? Kidnapping indeed! After I put my flipper down! And you're only doing it for security you need none of and prestige you can do without! Bad form, my dear."

But naiad-mother showed no remorse. She said that their son had been in no danger, that it had been a good character-building time for both young people, and had brought them measurably closer together (even though she didn't think it had).

Next month Soloonwa vanished from the forest. It was scoured low and high and in between, with no discovery. So the dryads held a séance and asked the spirits of their tree ancestors where the girl was. The leaves of the medium-tree, a southern beech, roared for near half an hour in the winds from the unseen world, and then the medium said, "She is on an island of cliffs in Lake Vaska Memu. And the one best suited to find and save her is—Merzan the naiad."

Merzan chuckled into his elbow, but nonetheless couldn't help feeling flattered. He prepared and set out, eastward, down the great river, white-foaming Ilwakalu. He had abundant adventures on the way to the lake. Once there he found it difficult climbing to the top of the cliffs. But a passing freshwater dolphin took him in his water form into his mouth, leapt up, and spat him up to the cliff-top.

The naiad then penetrated the labyrinth of spells woven over the island and rescued Soloonwa from a strange castle made of various metals. When, pursued by the fierce fire-boars of the place, they came to the cliff-edge, Merzan surrounded Soloonwa in his water form so she could jump from the cliff-top into the lake below without harming herself from the impact.

Then they made their way back to their beloved Lake Chellu country, being slightly delayed by only seven adventures.

But their feelings were unchanged.

"And to think of all the trouble I was put to to make this come about!" complained dryad-father one evening in an unguarded moment when Soloonwa was out—and so a similar scene played itself out in Dryad's Bower to that which had ensued between the naiad-parents following Merzan's return.

Shortly after, naiad-mother met dryad-father beside Market Pool on a busy day, and she said to dryad-father, "Your daughter rescued my son from peril, but no love came of it." And dryad-father said to naiad-mother, "Your son rescued my daughter from danger, but no love has resulted."

Naiad-mother replied, "The only thing that will work now is time and an absence of pressure."

So there matters were left.

The naiad and dryad families stopped trying to cajole, compel, or manipulate Merzan and Soloonwa into marriage. They thought this posture, plus time and the young people's progress in getting to know each other, would draw the couple together. But months and months, and seasons, went by, and still no love sprang up in the girl's and boy's hearts. Not amorous love, at least. They liked each other, certainly, and were excellent and worthy representatives of their people; but they were as far away from marrying as ever.

2.

Many among the clans of naiads and dryads at Lake Chellu prayed their son and daughter would get married; even though the clans had agreed to stop exerting pressure on them.

Their prayers fell on the ground and turned into soil.

But one naiad woman prayed that the son and daughter would find just what they needed, whatever that was.

Her prayer fell on the ground, but it turned into a caterpillar which crawled to a pine tree, climbed up its bark, and cocooned itself under a branch. In time it emerged as a moth: the great tree moth of the far Southern nights.

The moth fluttered through the starlit woods, wondering, "Where am I to go? What am I to do? I am, after all, a prayer."

Suddenly the moth felt an urge to fly east. She did, and came to an old unused well. She felt she must fly down it: which, despite trepidation, she did.

She flew down, down through the chill air, down through the cold water, down through the earth, into the seas of liquid stone that lie far beneath: for the well shaft ran all that way. It was a terribly arduous journey. She came to the domain of the pyrads, the fire-dwelling beings with seven sexes. She flew through their domain, looking at them, but rejecting first one, then another, then still another, and then yet more, till she had rejected 283,000 of them. But the 283,000th-and-first was different. She settled on its shoulder and whispered in its ear. Then she flew and landed on a nearby bush of white filaments, and looked at the pyrad. It was pausing, its flames still a minute. Then it shook itself, jumped, and rushed away toward the shaft down which the moth had come, and vanished up it.

The pyrad flew all the way up to the well-shaft's opening and came out of it and stood on the grass, dropping its temperature so as not to set fire to the wood.

Then it set off for the shore of Lake Chellu.

The moth, meanwhile, tried to take off from the bush of white filaments to follow the pyrad up the shaft. But she realized she had died on the journey to the pyrad's domain. The heat and pressure and lack of air had killed her. But she looked back on her life as a job well done. She fell off the branch and was absorbed in the domain of fire.

But part of her, which was like ice, was not, and this part flew back up the shaft into the night.

3.

The pyrad came amongst the naiad and dryad clans of the Lake Chellu districts, and dwelt among these peoples for several months. It did several remarkable things, and grew much admired and liked in that country.

For one thing, it could to an extent change its shape, and was able to turn at will into a brilliant fiery version of a naiad or a dryad.

"It is so much more attractive than all the dryad boys—and girls!" said Soloonwa.

"It is so much more admired for its appearance and personality than any of the naiad girls—and boys!" said Merzan.

"And what a fire-tree it can make!" cried Soloonwa. "It's more lovely than any of our dryad trees." Then she frowned.

"I notice it can dive deeper than naiads, probably even deeper than nereids. Its fire keeps it warm," said Merzan, flipping a stone into the lake with his tail.

The pyrad brought naiad-father his newspapers on time and helped him with his lake-bottom rock-garden, in which Merzan had not taken an interest for years.

"That's a fine boy," said naiad-father to naiad-mother one evening, laying aside his expensive magazine which was engraved on lovely thin slabs of stone.

"It's not a boy," said naiad-mother. "Pyrads have seven sexes!"

"Well he's a boy to me," said naiad-father, taking a puff of his steam-pipe.

The pyrad also was easily able to prune some of the great gnarled old trees in dryad-mother's forest garden, in which Soloonwa had not taken an interest since she was a little seedling. It also sometimes provided fires for heating or cooking without the need of any wood to burn, which impressed dryad-mother, and she said so to her husband.

There was a drought that summer, and the forest burned, which was a periodic necessity and was not opposed in general—but this was so unusually fierce a fire that it threatened the sanctuary groves of the dryads, and the naiads could not bring enough water to save them. But then the pyrad burned so hot that it sucked all the oxygen out of the forest round the sanctuary, and so asphyxiated and blocked the fire.

The pyrad was acclaimed throughout the Lake Chellu country.

But many of the naiads, including Merzan, were chagrinned and humbled at being unable to help much; and there was some grumbling about the fiery newcomer.

In fact, the pyrad was so excellent in matters both dryad and naiad that the naiad and dryad in question felt out in the cold.

Soon afterward, Merzan took his water form and poured himself into a hollow in a grove of monkey-puzzle trees. Though it was sunny, with golden shafts from the northern sky penetrating the foliage, the naiad's water was overcast.

And Soloonwa was there—he hadn't seen her at first—and she hung over the pool in her ash-form, looking up at herself from the water. And though it was summer, her leaves showed yellow and brown—not even the vivid reds and yellows of high autumn.

"I admire this pyrad," said Merzan, "but I am most tired, almost dried-out with hearing of her, him."

"And my leaves are falling nearly into the sere from a similar exhaustion," replied Soloonwa. "Though, yes, I certainly respect him, her." Then, "Is it not comic how our parents fall over themselves in praising the pyrad?" she added.

He chortled, which made circular ripples in his surface. "How my father loves it how he, she brings him his newspapers!" he remarked.

"Well, well, if the pyrad is pleasing our parents," said the dryad-girl, "we can act to please ourselves."

"And what would please you, dearest Soloonwa?" asked the naiad-boy, and though in water-form he had no lungs, he felt like he was holding his breath.

"The same thing that would please you, I fancy, my sweet Merzan," she replied.

"And what is that?"

She extended a root into the pool.

He clasped it.

"Oh good!" he cried. "Let us get married directly."

"Yes, let's!" she echoed.

How happy everyone was on the day and night of the marriage of Soloonwa Dryad's-daughter with Merzan the Naiad of First Clan Tharquem! And Merzan's mother and Soloonwa's father joyfully added an entry to the *Book of the Marriages of Wood and River* (or *River and Wood*, depending who you were).

And once they were wed, they discovered they really did love each other best after all. "It isn't just that we both cordially dislike the pyrad," they said.

And the new couple conceived a child under the moon.

But what that child was, and did—is another story of this land of Cothirya.

A Poem by David Sparenberg

The Holy Green of Time

In honor of Tom Bombadil

After the longest
Night
Dawn.

After the longest
Winter
Spring.

After the longest
fear
and loss
and sorrow
the bursting out
of Joy.

After the longest
dark, lingering
and imposing shadows
Light.

Faces flourish.
Flowers blossom.
An April robin
in new grass. The
Holy Green of Time. A
pollen dusted
honeybee….

Gratitude
is in bloom.
Rejoice!

Holly in the New Millennium

By Susan Cornford

Once upon a time Holly's grandmother used to fly about, playing hide and seek with the butterflies amongst the flowers. But that was then and now there was a whole new world with global warming that threatened flowers, butterflies and, ultimately, fairies of all sorts.

That was why they were holding this summit, with representatives of what humans called "supernatural" creatures from all over the world. Holly gazed around the fairy ring in the midst of the world's last great forest, pleased to see such a good turnout. She was not surprised to see a large contingent of yetis and sasquatches, as they inhabited the rapidly dwindling frozen places.

The meeting was called to order by Sylvia, the local wood nymph, and the very air grew heavier as each group reported in turn. Even the mermaids, represented by the Frog Prince, were already suffering from desalination of the seas.

Finally they put forward any ideas for solving the problem, which took them a great deal less time. In the end, they voted for a world-wide fly-over to scatter fairy dust. This was intended to enchant the humans so they would all start doing environmentally-friendly things.

All the supernatural folk who knew even a little bit of chemistry were tasked with making extra supplies of fairy dust. Others, like Pegasus and the unicorns, transported stockpiles to the distribution points. It was set for the next full moon to ensure the best visibility for complete coverage of the planet.

Holly lined up proudly to take on her load of fairy dust and filled all her special pockets; the amount was carefully calculated to be the maximum that she could carry and still get airborne. They'd all been doing strength and stamina exercises to be super fit. The signal was given, and they all took off and scattered every last grain of the fairy dust over the earth.

The only problem was that several large volcanos then erupted and this ended up blowing most of the fairy dust out into space. Who was to know that it would give Hades an allergic reaction and make him sneeze? So, it was back to the drawing board.

After a long debate, the leprechauns agreed to donate all their pots of gold to help the cause. Brian suggested that they post challenges for humans on social media, with rewards at the end of the rainbow, for implementing the best "green" product or technique. This was all set to be put into place when they realized that, no matter how much it rained, there were no rainbows appearing anywhere in the sky. An emergency session was called to which Iris was invited. She explained that all of her rainbows were still there; they just couldn't be seen because the colors had been bleached out by the fairy dust.

Nobody could think of a single other way to magically help overcome the problems of the environment that they shared with humans. So, they sadly went home to make the best of what they had left whilst it lasted.

Holly sat on her trademark hollyhock and swayed back and forth in the breeze, humming softly to herself. One of the human children was in the garden as well, playing with her doll that sat in a small chair, facing the girl. "Now, Eve, you must pay close attention! We are going to put out all of our solar panels to absorb the energy from the sun. Then we'll divide our rubbish into the proper bins for recycling as much as possible. Finally, we can water the flowers because it's our rostered day for doing it. Remember, it's our job to save the planet, so your children will have somewhere beautiful like this to play."

Not long after that, each human child on Earth was paired with a magical "advisor" from the local area. It was everyone's best chance to live happily ever after.

A Poem by Sarah Berti
You Passed Me the Story

in the dark
you passed me the story

it was blazing
a holy brand

the blaze was a story
in your hand

Rose Print by Leigh Ann Brook

Join the Mythopoeic Society!

Read our quarterly Newsletter, *MythPrint*!
→*included with membership*

Purchase copies of our scholarly journal, *MythLore*!
→*$15.00 electronic, $25+ for paper copies in the mail; 2 issues/year*

Subscribe to our creative writing journal, *The Mythic Circle*!
→*still $8.00 (2021) for one annual issue*

Attend our annual convention every late July/early August!
→*Usually located in smaller cities near larger universities*
→*2022 location: Albuquerque, NM*

Enroll in our first-ever Online Winter Seminar!
→*February 5, 2022; other details forthcoming*

Go to < http://www.mythsoc.org/join.htm >

The Mythopoeic Society is a non-profit international literary and educational organization for the study, discussion, and enjoyment of fantastic and mythic literature, especially the works of Tolkien, C.S. Lewis, and Charles Williams. The word "mythopoeic" (myth-oh-PAY-ik or myth-oh-PEE-ic), meaning "mythmaking" or "productive of myth", aptly describes much of the fictional work of the three authors who were also prominent members of an informal Oxford literary circle (1930s-1950s) known as the Inklings. We have been in continuous operation since 1967.

Aspiring Contributors:

Send stories, poems, and images (.docx/pdf/jpeg) to
mythiccircle@mythsoc.org

OR

Enroll with the MythSoc Digital Commons at SWOSU at

< https://dc.swosu.edu/ >

AND

Download Free Back Issues of
The Mythic Circle at

< https://dc.swosu.edu/mcircle/ >

AND while you're at it—

Check out our free audio files for Issue #42 (2020)

< https://dc.swosu.edu/mcircle/ >

→Scroll down and click on any story/poem title to access audio.

Made in the USA
Middletown, DE
12 September 2021

47684088R00046